Best Baseball Stories
A Quarter Century

Hank Lowenkron • Editor

tempo
books

GROSSET & DUNLAP, INC.
Publishers   New York

To my Wife, Ann
—One of the best sports I know.

CONTENTS

1
SANDY KOUFAX: ARTIST AT WORK

Have you ever watched an artist creating a picture with seemingly casual movements of his brush? What may look like a random stroke suddenly becomes a vital part of an appealing scene. Such was the experience of watching a sharp Sandy Koufax perform his masterpieces on the mound. After the 1966 season, the pain and treatments discussed in the following story became too much for Koufax, and he decided to end his playing career. The decision came after "Dandy" Sandy compiled a career-high total of 27 wins while losing only nine times. He did more than break the Cy Young jinx writer Charles Morey discusses. In fact, he shattered it; he won the award for a third time with the help of a 1.73 earned run average for 323 innings. He struck out 317 batters while leading the Dodgers to a National League championship. Koufax struck out 2,396 batters in his career and was tenth on the all-time list in that category at the start of the 1974 baseball season.

By Charles Morey

If America's sports idols constitute this country's royalty, then hand the crown and scepter to Sandy Koufax, the unquestioned king.

The stylish southpaw of the Los Angeles Dodgers looks the part. He is strikingly handsome with dark wavy hair, even features, a warm but reserved smile and at all times a gentleman. He acts the part. When Sandy takes the mound he rules supreme. There may be an iron fist in that velvet glove he wears but the important thing is, he never takes off the glove.

They call Sandy baseball's most eligible bachelor, but why limit it to the diamond sport? With a bow to Sinatra (not married at this writing), Koufax can be called the most eligible bachelor in the country, period. There is no greater catch than an unmarried king.

From time to time he comes into the sights of match-making mothers, friendly brothers with friendly sisters and friends who have friends. But so far Sandy has escaped, if you'll permit that word.

He has a standard gag to cover the matter. With a friendly but distant look at the many mothers who would love to be his mother-in-law Sandy says: "If anybody knows a lady doctor, that would make my mother happy."

At the age of 30, Sandy is at the peak of his pitching power. He is a cinch to draw paychecks totaling $100,000 from the Dodgers in 1966 and you can pad that out real good with side money from investments, endorsements, fees for personal appearances and the kind of added money that finds its way into a celebrity's bank account.

No man, not even a king of sports, escapes problems and Sandy has one that is real, earnest and potentially a crippling one. It is called arthritis. Sandy has it in his left elbow, the one he wheels and deals with.

He had to fight that, as well as the enemy hitters, from the opening pitch of the regular season in 1965 to the closing toss of the world series, which he delivered to make his second straight shutout of the Minnesota Twins official.

Before every game of the regular season in 1965, Sandy had to sit for a long and irritating rubbing of his pitching arm in which a stinging ointment was applied to the skin to stimulate it. After every game Koufax had to cool his hot wing with ice in a long cellophane bag.

They wrote him off in April as a part-time pitcher. In July they said, "He's ready for Medicare." By September they were shaking their heads in amazement at his stamina and fortitude. In October the Twins shook their heads in dismay after they beat him once and he bounced back to blank them twice.

"His curve ball doesn't look good to me," said San Francisco Giant pitcher Bob Shaw in July after Sandy hung a 2-1 loss on the Giants.

"I got the feeling Sandy was hurrying the game so he could rest his sore arm," this from Cookie Lavagetto, coach of the San Francisco club.

Sore arm, Cookie? All the Giant pitchers should have them. Throw these figures into a computer in the Giant front office. A season record of 26 victories and eight losses. No National League lefty ever won more games in a single season.

A total of 382 strikeouts, breaking Bob Feller's record. Twenty-seven complete games, nobody in the league had as many. A run of eleven straight victories at a key point of the campaign, the longest streak of the year.

A perfect game, the first since Don Larsen's in the 1956 world series. It came on September 9th against the Chicago Cubs at a time when the arthritis was clutching at his arm like a hungry eagle hunting food for hungry eaglets.

When Sandy finished with the Cubs, a veteran member of that team said to two rookies, Don Young and Byron Browne who had just played their first major league game, "Are you two guys sure you still want to play in this league?"

It was Sandy's fourth no-hitter. Nobody else has ever pitched that many. He no-hitted the Mets in 1962 which may be the same as gunning canaries in a cage. But he hung one on the hard-swinging Giants in 1963, on the slashing Phillies in '64, and in '65 it was the Cubs.

Minnesota beat him in the second game of the series, which, coming hard on the heels of their decision over Don Drysdale in the opener, seemed to give the Twins a lock on the blue ribbon. But Drysdale recovered to halt Minnesota in the fourth game after Claude Osteen stopped the Dodger skid in game number three. Koufax shut out the Twins, 7-0, in the fifth contest, had two days to rest his arthritic elbow and after Minnesota won game six, Sandy blanked them, 2–0, for all the money in the seventh game.

That second game in Minnesota, in which he pitched six innings and gave up two of the five runs the Twins scored, flawed a remarkable world series string for Sandy.

He pitched two games in 1963 against the Yankees and won them both as the Los Angeles Club blitzed the Bombers in four games. Sandy made little gentlemen of the Bronx Buckos by fanning 15 of them in the opener, an all-time series record. He also won the fourth game after Johnny Podres and Don Drysdale took care of games two and three.

It began for Sandy in 1955 when the Dodgers signed him as a bonus pitcher for a price estimated from $14,000 to $30,000. The Dodgers were still in Brooklyn and for his first six seasons Sandy was rated one of the fastest, wildest, and potentially greatest flingers in the majors.

But potential and promise need polish. Sandy was slow to get it. He might be waiting yet if it wasn't for a second-string catcher named Norm Sherry who sat next to the Brooklyn-born southpaw on a plane ride to an exhibition game in 1961.

"Sandy," said Sherry, "why don't you stop trying to throw the ball past every hitter you face? Take just a little off it."

Sandy did. The little he took off left a lot still on it. He won 18 games while losing 13 in 1961, an excellent record, and led the league in strikeouts with 269.

The erratic thrower had become a stylish southpaw. By 1962 he had become that priceless pitcher, the stopper. It was that summer that saw him hit hard by a curious circulatory ailment in a finger on his pitching hand. It sent him out of action for ten weeks. That was the year the Dodgers lost the pennant to San Francisco by one game, the deciding one in a three-game playoff. No computer is necessary to figure what the outcome would have been if Koufax had not had his circulatory ailment.

The prophets of doom were writing him off again for the 1963 season. Sandy silenced their voices and dried their pens by pitching the Dodgers to the National League pennant and a sweep of the world series.

That won him his first Cy Young Award, the trophy given each year to the outstanding pitcher in the big leagues. Sandy won it for the second time in '65, a fact which is putting him eye to eye with a mild jinx. Only once in ten years has a Cy Young winner come back to win 20 games the next season. Only the irrepressible Warren Spahn slumped (slumped??) to 19 victories in 1964 after his '63 award when his arm kicked up again.

Spahn, in a way, represents a goal for Sandy. The all-time leader of southpaws, Warren had 363 victories through the 1965 season. Now 30, Sandy had 138 at the close of play in '65. He has a long way to go to catch the wily Warren.

For one thing, Spahn won 108 games in his first six years on the big wheel. Sandy had 36 after six campaigns. For another, Spahn had an arm that was three parts rubber and one part steel. He didn't know what a sore arm was. Koufax has had to grapple with both that numbing circulatory ailment and the painful arthritic elbow.

Neither difficulty is calculated to improve with the aging process. In fact, the physician who takes care of Sandy's elbow, Dr. Robert K. Kerlan, orthopedic specialist, is fearful of a flare-up at any time.

"It wouldn't have surprised me if Sandy had to lay off for an extended period at any time in 1965," said the doctor, "and something like that could happen in 1966. I'll put it this way. Interference with his normal schedule is a probability. Continuing with his normal schedule can be classed as a possibility."

Like anybody else who is burdened with something chronic, Koufax has learned to live with his arthritis. He takes a powerhouse pill the day before he pitches, the day he pitches and the day after he works. That doesn't leave him free of pills very often. The pill is a brand of phenylbutazone, an anti-inflammatory agent which can be taken only under rigid medical administration. The capsule reduces inflammation. Sandy is a faithful patient.

Sandy is philosophical about his ailment and his future

in baseball, which with good health could stretch for more than another decade. He says in matter of fact tones, "It could end at any time. I got away with it in 1965. It could be that I won't get away with it in 1966."

The doctor says the arthritis was years in the making and the good doctor surely knows what he is talking about. But there was an incident that seemed to trigger it. Early in August of 1964, Sandy injured his elbow while sliding into a base in a game with the Cards. The elbow swelled but Sandy took his regular turn on the mound and managed to win two more games until the arm ballooned to the point where he could pitch no more. His victory total for the year had reached 19. He never did reach 20.

You can tell a lot about a ball player by what other athletes say about him.

Before the 1963 world series the proud Yankees were amused, on the surface at least, by the predictions that Sandy's fast ball would knock the bats from their hands.

"He's all we've been reading about," snorted Mickey Mantle on the morning of the opening game and then added sarcastically, "guess we don't have much chance against him."

"He's every bit as good as he reads," commented a thoughtful Mickey after Koufax fanned 15 Yankees while winning the opener.

"It was a helluva pitch," said Mickey, by then a believer, after he took a called third strike with the tying run on base in the last inning of the fourth game as Sandy won his second of the series. "I thought sure it was going to be too high and then it broke four feet on me."

Of all the words, millions in number, which have been written or spoken about Sandy, the most sincere and certainly the most succinct were voiced by Ken Boyer, now of the Mets and a couple of years ago the most valuable player in the National League while playing third base for St. Louis.

"Koufax," said Boyer after losing to him one day, "is just too damned much."

2
BROOKS ROBINSON: HUMAN VACUUM CLEANER

Some time in the future Brooks Robinson will be voted into Baseball's Hall of Fame. The only question is when. To be selected as one of the game's immortals, a player usually must be retired for five years. That seems unlikely to happen to Brooks. In 1974 the Baltimore third baseman celebrated his thirty-seventh birthday by batting .288, his top mark since 1965. He was still handling nearly every ball hit in his direction and playing in nearly every game.

Robinson didn't take the fourth game of the 1970 Series off, as jokingly suggested here by Phil Jackman. He played in the game, won by Cincinnati, 6-5. However, don't blame Brooks for the outcome. He had a home run, scored twice and had three singles in going four-for-four with the bat. Perhaps the biggest reason for the Reds' win was their good sense in not hitting the ball towards Baltimore's third baseman. Brooks was named the top player in the series after the Orioles won the fifth game. For the Series, Brooks batted .429, with nine hits in 21 at bats.

By Phil Jackman

The Oriole third baseman could have overslept and missed the fourth game of the World Series today and it

Copyright 1970, **The Evening Sun,** Baltimore, Md.

7

wouldn't have mattered, the 1970 showdown had already been named the Brooks Robinson Story.

For the third game in a row yesterday, The Man did things with the glove and bat that had 51,773 stadium watchers and a few more than that looking in on the tube gaping in amazement. Even a kid with a Jules Verne imagination couldn't dream up the Series Brooks has already had.

And you get the impression he's beginning to realize it. "It is strange," he said, "having the opportunity to make plays three games in a row like that. Sometimes you go a week without a tough play."

After watching B. Robby bash a two-run double in the first inning to get the Birds started toward a 9–3 victory behind Dave McNally, Cincinnati's Sparky Anderson sighed, "Robinson continues to do it in the field . . . and now he's doing it with his bat."

It wasn't what Sparky said, it was the way he said it. Resignation fairly dripped from his words. "If the Orioles win the Series and he doesn't get the car as the Most Valuable Player, they should have a total investigation."

Brooks had a second double to go with his clutch belt in the first inning, but these hits paled next to the three home runs the O's stroked, including a grand slam by McNally, and his daily test of your credulity afield.

This latest bit of larceny occurred in the sixth inning and involved Johnny Bench, who has to be thinking he's as snake-bit as teammate Lee May about now.

In the first two games, Robinson made masterpieces that not only robbed May of base hits but the Reds of much-needed runs. One was a backhanded stop and blind, over-the-shoulder throw from Section 27, Riverfront Stadium, Cincinnati, the second a diving stop and subsequent double play on a ball that should have been a double.

Cincy was still within hailing distance, trailing 4–1, when Bench bashed a liner into left field . . . wait a minute, Brooks has it with a headlong leap into the dust.

Earlier, Dave Johnson had made a diving grab of a Pete Rose belt the Reds' right fielder figured was good for three bases. "Defensively, they're so fine," Anderson pointed out, "that it doesn't matter where you hit the ball.

"Rose said he would have had a triple up the alley on the ball Johnson caught. Then again, Blair might have cut it off, who knows?"

"It wouldn't have got to the fence," the Orioles' center fielder assured. "Fact, I was thinking single if Davey didn't get to it."

So much for defense, except to say Rex Barney came up with the best line of the day when he was asked if B. Robby was back in the clubhouse following TV interviews: "He's not at his locker yet, but four guys are over there interviewing his glove."

This was an offensive game, from the rockets which kept leaving the premises while the home team was at bat to the fierce liners the Reds kept hitting and the O's kept catching.

Baltimore never trailed, which is an oddity in this Series, but it was never out of danger until McNally became the first pitcher in the history of October to bust a grand slam. It was the 12th Series slam and the first by a guy from Montana.

The other homer strokers for the Birds were Frank Robinson, a mammoth shot fielded by one of Baltimore's finest beyond the hedge in dead center, and Don Buford, who reached the bleachers beyond the 360 sign in right.

Considering that McNally's homer went to left, the Birds got great dispersion on their fifth, sixth and seventh circuit smashes of the test.

While Brooks Robby passes off what happened in last year's Series as "one of those things—a calamity of errors," something he did very early this season suggests otherwise, although he denies it.

Emblazoned across Brooks's suitcase all summer has been the identification strip: "Brooks Robinson, Baltimore Orioles, 1970 World Champions."

"I put that on there in April before our first road trip," the third baseman said. "I don't know why, I just did it."

It being done he no doubt figured he had to make good on the claim after going 1-for-19 against the Mets. "I al-

ways wish I had done more against New York," he admits,
and now it's Cincinnati paying the price.

3
PEE WEE AND JACKIE:
MORE THAN TEAMMATES

One of the most resonant events in baseball
took place when Branch Rickey picked Jackie
Robinson to become the first black playing as
a professional with whites. In this story readers
get an intimate look at the Hall of Famer with
the help of former Dodger shortstop Pee Wee
Reese and Joe Donnelly's skill. Robinson died
in 1972, but his contribution lives on.

By Joe Donnelly

Say Pee Wee Reese, and another era of Dodger fan
comes alive. Reese was a shortstop who filled the position
gracefully for the better part of two decades. His skills had
whispered thin when the Dodgers moved to the West Coast
in 1958 and that was his final season. The sweet class he
wore on and off the field never thinned.

Memories were rekindled yesterday when Reese was re-
united here with Jackie Robinson. Robinson was at a mid-
town restaurant to be honored as Sport Magazine's "Man
of the 25 Years." Reese was there from his Louisville
home because, well, he wanted to be there. That reflects
the bond existing between the two men; both are 52.

Robinson is white-haired and bent some with the years
that Reese wears so well. But go back 25 years through
Reese's eyes and see a Robinson that is vibrant and understand what yesterday was all about. The way he sees the
award, it was for Robinson's contribution to sports beyond

playing excellence. "I think he's deserving of it," the ex-shortstop said. "No matter what else I say, that's most significant."

Reese, the white man who dared to accept Robinson, who dared to see baseball's black pioneer as a man, along with few other teammates, didn't start out that way. Recalling his initial reaction, it illustrates how difficult something is that is now taken for granted.

"I was on a ship coming home from Guam for discharge in 1946," Reese said, "when they first told me that Mr. (Branch) Rickey had signed a black. A Southerner, I said, 'No way.' When they told me he (Robinson) was a shortstop, which Jackie was at first, I knew they had to be kidding."

There was to be room and pennants enough for both of them. Again, though, Reese wasn't convinced when he first saw Robinson on a ball field. "I had my doubts if he'd make it. He didn't have what you would call nice and easy hands in the field. He kind of stabbed at the ball."

Reese recalls the Dodgers training in Ciudad Trujillo (now Santo Domingo) rather than Florida, Robinson's first spring with the parent club ('47). "That was supposed to make it easier on him. But you still had to come north. In those days it was a slow process [barnstorming]. I think it was Birmingham where he got letters: 'You'll get shot if you step in to hit.' He stepped in to hit. In Fort Worth they hollered 'watermelon eater' and such at him."

Actually it started before that. Reese can remember a petition circulated by some Dodger teammates calling for Robinson's removal or the team wouldn't take the field. The shortstop told them to forget it, that there was no way he was going to sign it.

What had changed Reese from his initial reaction? "After being with him, playing cards with him, seeing his class, putting myself in his place." His place? "Yes, in a way," Reese said. "I tried to think of what it would be like for me breaking into a black league. I don't now how he did it without saying anything for two years. They threw at him quite a bit. But it was what they yelled at him. You knew he was an aggressive person just by the way he played and it had to be tearing at his guts."

The few like Reese—Clem Labine and Carl Erskine were other teammates who made it known they respected Robinson's struggle—made it a bit easier. "Sometimes you would try kidding with him to ease the situation," Reese recalled. "After he got the letters threatening to shoot him, I remember saying to him when we got in the field: Would you move over? Don't stay so close. The guys hollering 'watermelon eater' I'd holler back at, and they'd soon be on me almost as much as Jackie."

Robinson has his own special memory of helpful friendship the shortstop provided. "The Boston Braves didn't get on me the way the Phillies did," he said. "Some of theirs were the worst. But there was this time in Boston early and some of the Braves were hollering things while we were taking infield. I think they thought Pee Wee would react as a Southerner.

"Instead he came over and put his arm on my shoulder. I don't remember what he said. I doubt Pee Wee recalls. But it was the gesture. That said it all: Yell and scream as much as you want, we're a team. That's the way I recall that moment. And we were a team that was to win six pennants in 10 years. I think of today and can't help but think if we take a page out of Pee Wee Reese's book America would succeed."

It was Robinson up there accepting the award ". . . bestowed on me because I played a role that was created by a great man [Rickey] and supported by thousands." One of the thousands, the one who played next to him, sat in the background. "I don't normally go out to these things," Reese had said. "I felt I had to come to this."

There were other awards, a passel of the great ones gathered—John Unitas, pro football; Bill Russell, pro basketball; Kareem Jabbar, college basketball; Bob Mathias, track and field; Rod Laver, tennis, etc. They didn't give Reese an award. They didn't have to. He got his a long time ago.

4
ROGER MARIS: THE MAN WITH AN ASTERISK

A successful baseball player often finds someone chasing him with a pencil and notebook, tape recorder, or microphone. Learning to live with this fact is an occupational hazard. Few, however, have been pursued like Roger Maris as he battled to top the famed Babe Ruth's standard of 60 home runs in a single season. Maris hit 61 homers in 1961, but Baseball Commissioner Ford Frick elected to put an asterisk next to his feat because the schedule was longer. Maury Allen wrote the following story in 1968 after Maris had been traded to the St. Louis Cardinals and was in the process of closing out his career. After his record-setting year, Maris never came close to 40 homers. To this day he still becomes annoyed when he thinks about the boos he received in Yankee Stadium during 1962 while hitting "only" 33 homers and batting .256. The Yankee fans, many of whom felt Maris betrayed them by hitting more homers in a season than Ruth, ridiculed him even more in later years as his home run production fell and his batting average dipped. Still, Maris had the last word as he helped St. Louis win two straight National League titles before retiring.

By Maury Allen

After all the sound and fury, the boos, the cheers, the

quotes, the misquotes, Roger Maris ends his New York baseball career this weekend in Shea as the right fielder on another pennant-winning team. The Cardinals will be back next year. Maris won't.

"I'm just tired of baseball," Maris said the other night in St. Louis.

Maris, at 34, will move his family to the sun of Gainesville, Florida, travel an eight-county area as a beer distributor, get in a few more rounds of golf, and not once miss the drudgery, the aches, the cruel schedule, and the pressures of professional baseball. Maris never really loved playing baseball, the way Mickey Mantle loves it or Willie Mays or Pete Rose. It was his job, his profession, his way of earning $75,000 a year for his family. Now he simply moves to a new job.

"I won't miss baseball," he said. "I'll have a job that will keep me busy, and I'll be able to come home to my family every night."

Maris stood in front of his locker the other night in St. Louis and seemed at peace with himself. Another month and another week in October and it will be over. After 16 years as a professional ball player and seven pennants, Maris can take off his uniform with pride. He has done his share.

It is seven years since Maris hit his 61 in '61, since he turned the country on, since he rescued baseball from its depression, since he stood each day before a growing crowd of reporters to answer the embarrassing and the inane questions, the important and the unimportant, the nonsense and the trivia.

"I didn't mind '61," he said, as he was reminded of that memorable year for the umpteenth time, "it was '62 I didn't like."

It was in 1961 that the generation gap first showed its head. The Establishment ruled that 162 games was something different and Babe Ruth must be saved for posterity. How ridiculous. If only Ruth had been around himself to disagree with such foolishness.

"A season's a season," said Maris. "Nobody came

around and asked me if I wanted to play a 154-game season or 162."

The Establishment gave him the asterisk but the baseball fans gave him the record. No one, not Babe Ruth, not anybody, ever hit 61 homers in one season. Maybe nobody ever will again.

"Hitting goes in cycles," said Maris. "Nobody thought Ruth's record would ever be broken. Home-run hitters will come along again. Maybe next year, maybe in 10 years. That's the way the game is."

Maris is not an emotional person. When he puts on his baseball suit, he is a man at work. He is thinking of his beer business now. Maybe in 10 or 20 years he will grow old enough to become nostalgic and romantic about the summer of 1961.

Maybe he will remember the drama, the excitement, the nervous tension of an entire population pulling for him or against him, never once ignoring him. He caused arguments in barrooms and living rooms, sons debated fathers and daughters became aware of baseball with mothers. Was a season a season? Was Ruth's record inviolate? Who was this guy named Maris anyway?

He was a 26-year-old Yankee right fielder who thrilled every kid who saw him, excited every fan who watched him, moved every sports writer who wrote about him.

There was the day in Baltimore, 58 home runs counted, game No. 154. He needed two to catch Ruth under Establishment rules. He lined out in front of the wall. He homered for 59. He lined out again. He was caught by Hoyt Wilhelm's knuckler and dribbled a ball back to the mound.

The Baltimore crowd stood on its feet and cheered his effort. This was Babe Ruth country and Maris had won them over. They seemed ashamed they had rooted against him. A few days later he hit Jack Fisher for number 60 and then Tracy Stallard for number 61.

The home crowd at Yankee Stadium yelled itself wild with pleasure. Maris made it to the top step of the dugout and John Blanchard pushed him out front. The crowd got louder and louder and louder.

Maris is a private man. He had only done his job. He

did not quite understand the turmoil. The people in the stands were telling him they were with him. Damn the record books and the asterisks and Ford Frick and the Roaring Twenties. This was now and here, and he had given them something for their own lives, their own memories, the glory of their own times.

Maybe Roger Maris never had Babe Ruth's wave and smile, but Babe Ruth never had as many home runs in one summer as Roger Maris. No man could ever change that. It was a summer none of us shall ever forget.

So long, Roger, and thanks.

5
FRANK ROBINSON: MULTITALENTED PERFORMER

Even if Frank Robinson had not become the first black manager in the history of major-league baseball he would still be one of the game's immortals. No other man has been named the Most Valuable Player in both leagues. In his prime Robinson was the type of player who could produce victory using either his bat or his glove, his legs or his arms. A keen mind made him an even bigger asset too for whatever club employed him. It's interesting that in this 1971 story Joe Heiling mentions predictions that Frank Robinson would be the first black manager—three years before Cleveland made it happen. Robinson's experience as a player came in handy towards victory in the game described in the story, but it only postponed a victory celebration for Pittsburgh. The Pirates took the decisive seventh game, 2-1, with Steve Blass pitching a four-hitter. A home run by Roberto Clemente helped

make the Bucs a champion, but that's another
story, included elsewhere in this book.

By Joe Heiling

The flattest feet in baseball tied up the 1971 World
Series Saturday afternoon.

They belong to 36-year-old Frank Robinson, and he
urged them on with dirt-pounding haste in the tenth inning,
sliding home on Brooks Robinson's sacrifice fly as the Baltimore Orioles leveled the Pittsburgh Pirates, 3–2.

This was the game the Birds had to win or call it a season. They had to force a dramatic seventh game showdown
and the Robinson boys did it as the O's used three 20-game
winners on the mound.

The beginning of the end for the Bucs came on reliefer
Bob Miller's one-out walk to Frank Robinson in the first
extra-inning game since 1969.

Robby's arches have fallen. His knees ache, and the
Achilles tendon in his right ankle throbbed louder than a
bass fiddle. "My feet are flat," he said, "but they're great."

Indeed they are.

When Merv Rettenmund sent a hopping single up the
middle, Frank was off and running. The hit was past
Miller, the fourth Buc hurler, before he could react, and
all eyes followed the bouncing ball.

Second baseman Dave Cash sprinted to a spot back of
the bag and it eluded his glove by the barest of margins.
Shortstop Jackie Hernandez, straining for all he was worth,
couldn't cut it off, either.

Once Robby saw it was going through, his mind was
made up. He never broke stride as he rounded second, hit
the bag with one foot and set sail for third base.

He dived into the bag ahead of Vic Davalillo's throw,
got to his feet and waited for Brooks to drive him home.
This the Orioles' popular veteran did, lifting a fly ball to
Davalillo, who had pinch hit in the top of the tenth and
remained in the game to play center.

There were Birds on first and third with one out, and the crowd of 44,174 could sense it was all over.

Frank Robinson tagged up as Davalillo hauled in Brooks' drive in short center. He should have thrown the man out at home plate.

But Davalillo's peg was to the left of the plate and catcher Manny Sanguillen was forced to hustle about six feet up the line. The ball took one kangaroo hop and Sanguillen leaped for possession of it.

As he did, Robinson threw himself at the plate, flipping Sanguillen in the process. Earl Weaver, the O's manager, was one of the first to reach the smiling Robby as he looked up out of the dirt.

"He was straddling the line," said Robby, the man many predict will be the first black manager in the major leagues. "The ball took a high hop and he had to go up and I hit his legs."

When Brooks walked up to take his cuts, he knew what he wanted to do. Hit a fly ball, not dump anything on the grass that could turn into a double play.

"I probably lead the league in hitting into double plays," he was able to joke later. "I'm not the fastest man alive, you know."

His fondest hope was for a pitch he could step into—slap a solid piece of the bat on.

"The pitcher (Miller) didn't want a fly ball," said Brooks, "and he jammed me pretty good, but I got enough of it. I kept looking at Frank to see if he was going. The ball wasn't that deep. When I saw Frank go I was glad."

Thus ended one of the finest Series games played in many a moon.

Dave McNally hadn't worked on relief since July 19, 1969, but he emerged the winner after Jim Palmer had yielded both runs and eight hits in nine innings and Pat Dobson had come on in the tenth.

McNally faced just two batters. Davalillo lined out to begin the tenth, but Dave Cash singled and stole second— the Pirates' fifth theft in three games—as Hebner was whiffing.

This left first base open and Clemente, 11-for-25, was walked intentionally.

"Dave stole it on his own," said Danny Murtaugh, that Irish kisser of his unsmiling. "But that doesn't bother me because it brought up (Willie) Stargell. I'll take my chances on a 125-RBI man any time."

Although 4-for-20 in the Series, Stargell is a formidable figure at home plate. McNally pitched him carefully and walked the big slugger before Al Oliver flied out, leaving the Series knotted at three wins apiece.

The Orioles go into Sunday's final game—at 1 P.M., CDT—at a serious disadvantage. They're down to their last 20-game winner, Mike Cuellar. He'll be opposed by Steve Blass, the Bucs 15-game winner who subdued the O's 5-1 on three hits in the third game to trigger his team's comeback.

"I'm happy to pitch the seventh game," said the candid Pittsburgh right-hander. "Now I get a chance to win the car (presented annually to the Series' outstanding performer)."

The Orioles, to a man, wanted to jump into an early lead in Game 6. It didn't work out that way.

In the second inning, Oliver doubled and scored on Bob Robertson's single. Then Clemente, within two hits of the Series record of 13, slashed an opposite-field homer to right off Palmer in the third.

Protecting the 2-0 lead was the responsibility of Bob Moose, the sixth different starter Murtaugh has employed in six games. Moose made a good run at it, allowing just one hit—Don Buford's opening single—through four innings.

Brooks Robinson singled in the fifth and Mark Belanger later drew the second of his three walks. The threat was mild with the pitcher up. Palmer struck out.

They had been scoreless for 22 innings.

The momentum began to shift in the sixth. Buford's towering home run to right left the O's down by one run.

After Richie Hebner's error and Boog Powell's single, Moose made his exit and Bob Johnson, loser in Game 2, became his replacement. Runners were on first and third with nobody out, but Johnson refused to wilt, retiring the next three Birds.

He wasn't as fortunate in the seventh when Dave Johnson's single tied it up.

Belanger singled with one away and stole second. When the count went to 3-and-1 on Buford, after Palmer struck out, Dave Guisti put in his third appearance of the Series.

He completed the walk and Johnson, the ex-Texas Aggie, dropped a hit into left field, to make it 2–2 and take your pick.

After this, Guisti did his job. And he did it well, keeping the Birds off the scoreboard before leaving for Davalillo, the pinch hitter. Miller, the well-traveled reliever, was deputized to pitch the tenth.

It wasn't a fearful assignment, merely a tense one. The Birds collected only nine hits in three games in Pittsburgh and the Pirates out-hit them in this one, nine to eight.

"We didn't exactly kill the ball today," said Frank Robinson with a sly grin.

And he was right. The Bucs were done in by a pair of flat feet and a fly ball to center that traveled just far enough. And a throw from the outfield that was off the mark.

6
A LOOK AT BASEBALL

Have you ever wondered why baseball is the national sport of the United States? If you take the time to read this selection you should find the answer. Ray Fitzgerald of **The Boston Globe** uses few words, but provides lasting thoughts.

By Ray Fitzgerald

Maybe you think, from what you've read over the winter, that baseball was born in a lawyer's office, grew up in a courtroom and flourishes in a bookmaker's shop.

That's not so. Baseball is more than Bowie Kuhn, Curt Flood, Marvin Miller and Dennis McLain. It's more than franchise shifts and lawsuits.

Baseball is grace and talent under pressure. It's Carl Yastrzemski scooping up a single on the gallop in left field at Fenway and throwing the tying run out at the plate.

It's Frank Howard missing and the crowd going "Oooooh," and Howard three innings later hitting the ball 450 feet.

It's Harmon Killebrew's tape-measure homer into the center-field stands and Rico Petrocelli with his short swing sending the ball 316 feet into the left-field screen.

Baseball is Bert Campaneris stealing third on a pitchout, George Scott turning a line drive into a double play. It's a Frank Robinson triple and Sam McDowell's fast ball.

Baseball is also excitement off the field. It's cops on horseback and crowds milling around the players' entrance.

It's kids leaning on a dugout before a game, yelling, "Yaz, gimme a autograph." It's a guy in the bleachers with a beer asking, "Why do they leave the bum in?" and a lady in a box seat asking, "Why don't they take the bum out?"

Baseball is watching the scoreboard for out-of-town results, and fighting for a ball with five people you've never seen before.

It's leaving your seat in the ninth when your team is five runs behind, but lingering in the runway to watch because somehow you think they'll pull victory out.

For a sports writer, baseball is a bunch of memories, most of which have little to do with runs, hits and errors.

It is 10,000 people at an airport to greet a team, and 1,000 people in a Cleveland Stadium that seats 80,000. It is Russ Gibson being told he is not going to make the club and Mike Derrick being told that he is.

It is Tom Satriano standing in a Washington hotel lobby holding his two-week-old baby, no bigger than a show box, and it's Mrs. Jerry Stephenson in a bikini, stopping traffic at the Ranch House Motel swimming pool in Winter Haven.

Baseball is writing 20 paragraphs in 20 minutes in order to catch a plane to Cleveland, and paying two dollars for one egg, three strips of bacon and some toast in the hotel coffee shop in New York.

The game is a chance to meet nice guys like Brooks Robinson, spoiled kids like Tony Horton and churls like Leo Durocher.

Baseball is contrast. It's Sparky Lyle throwing his glove in a trash barrel after giving up a game-winning grand slam, and it's Sparky Lyle surrounded by reporters after striking out the side with the bases loaded.

There is plenty wrong with baseball. Club owners are autocratic and players are greedy. The season is too long and the hot dogs are terrible.

A critic once characterized baseball as six minutes of action crammed into two and one-half hours.

Okay, I'll buy that. Much of the beauty of the game is in the mind of the beholder. What if the batter walks? Will he steal? Can he squeeze? Is the pitcher tired? Can the man pinch-hit? There is plenty of nonaction.

Nonetheless, you can have your blue lines, red dogs and double dribbles. Tomorrow the best of sports in a sports-crazy country returns to Fenway Park and I'll eat a hot dog if it kills me.

7
THE SHOT HEARD
ROUND THE WORLD

There is no other city in the world that can match New York when it comes to diversification of heritage, economic conditions and loyalties. Thus, in 1951 joy in upper Manhattan came at the expense of heartbreak and disbelief only a few miles away. Truth is often harder to believe than fiction! That's why any

Dodger fan who lived through it needs no reminder to recall the pain of hearing the late Russ Hodges wildly tell his listeners, "The Giants win the pennant, the Giants win the pennant." The pictures of that October afternoon are still vivid: Andy Pafko trying to push the wall back in the Polo Grounds, Eddie Stanky going wild on the field and Ralph Branca trying to hide himself in the sullen Dodger clubhouse and pleading with newsmen, "Leave me alone, please leave me alone." Branca remained in the majors until 1956, but he won only eight games and lost 12 in the three years after unwillingly placing his name in baseball's history book for eternity.

By John P. Carmichael

They've just carried Bobby Thomson off the field, swaying and bobbing on a sea of lurching shoulders. Fans have helped Leo Durocher to his feet where Eddie Stanky wrestled him down in the coaching box at third base.

The Polo Grounds is a little world gone mad, as up in the press-coop limp fingers try to set down the story-book finish to the most breathless pennant race in baseball history.

It's all over, finally, and the Giants play the Yankees tomorrow in the first game of the 1951 World Series.

The saga of their triumph will live forever, etched in those golden minutes of the ninth inning, with the score 4-2 against them, runners on second and third and Thomson virtually the last hope of a cause that was all but lost.

The horseshoe stands of the Polo Grounds seemed to hunch forward under the surge of 34,328 fans as Ralph Branca, summoned in relief for starter Don Newcombe, went into his windup and flung a called strike past the immobile Giant third baseman.

The ball went back to him again, and once more Branca drew himself up and let fly.

The pennant rode on the pitch. It rode into the left-field stands about 30 feet fair, and the last vestige of that 13½-game Dodger lead as of Aug. 12 vanished beyond recall in the doom of a 5-4 defeat only two putouts from what could have been Brooklyn's sixth flag in the last 35 years.

The whole story is out of fairyland's top drawer.

How the Giants won 37 of their last 44 games to gain a permanent tie the last day of the season.

How they won the first playoff game and then were humiliated in a 10-0 defeat.

How they battled from behind today to wipe out a 1-0 lead in the seventh inning, only to have their hopes crushed with a three-run Dodger rally in the eighth.

A year from now, or a hundred years from now, nobody will remember how they came out against the Yankees, even if they win.

The red-letter day in Giant history will be this Oct. 3, when they finally climbed the highest mountain and looked down on the shuttered city of Brooklyn, lying at their feet.

There was nobody out in the ninth when Alvin Dark and Don Mueller singled to put men on first and third.

Monte Irvin, the league's leader in runs-batted-in, popped out.

But "Whitey" Lockman doubled off the left-field wall, sending Dark home to make the score 4-2 against them, with the winning run at the plate.

Thomson had driven in the first Giant run, but he'd spoiled a promising rally in the second by faulty base-running.

The Dodger strategists, led by Charlie Dressen, decided that Newcombe had been around long enough. He had pitched a gritty game, but brilliant fielding saved him time and again.

So this was where Branca came in, who now goes down in history as the first man ever to lose three playoff games, including one in 1946 and one last Monday.

And this was where Thomson hit the three-run homer that will echo around the world as long as there is a world.

Maglie was wild from the outset. Of his first 14 pitches, only four were strikes, three on Furillo, after which he walked Reese and Snider.

As Jansen began warming up in the Giant bullpen, Robinson hit a first pitch for a single to left, scoring Reese.

Pafko hit to Thomson who stepped on third to force Snider, but missed the double play. However, Thomson took Hodges' foul near the stands.

The next three Dodgers, in the second inning, didn't get a ball out of the infield.

But Newcombe had throttled the Giants until, with Irvin gone in the second, Lockman shot a single between Hodges and Robinson. Thomson singled to left.

He saw Lockman round second and apparently thought he was headed for third. Thomson dashing toward second, was cut down, Pafko-Reese-Hodges, trying to regain first. Then Pafko went almost to the wall for Mays' drive and the threat was over.

They turned the lights on, presumably for Thomson, at the start of the third and Maglie took advantage of the greater visibility to set down Furillo, Reese and Snider in order.

Westrum walked to open the Giant half but was forced by Maglie on an attempted sacrifice. Reese was dumped by the sliding Westrum but held Newcombe's low throw.

Then Cox made a fine pickup of Stanky's smash behind third and turned it into a double play.

By now, Newcombe and Maglie had settled down to a tight duel and it wasn't until Cox beat out a bunt along the first base line to open the fifth that the Dodgers had another scoring chance.

Walker was allowed to hit and fanned. Newcombe failed to bunt twice and eventually forced Cox via Lockman and Furillo flied to Irvin.

After Reese had thrown out Lockman in the home half, Thomson skimmed a double just inside the third-base line.

The third hit off Maglie was Snider's single to left in the sixth after Reese whiffed. But the "Duke" was out trying to steal.

Robinson walked, but Pafko popped out.

The Giants had the top of their batting order up but they went down one-two-three, thanks to a fine stop by Cox of Dark's elusive hopper.

After a run of 16 consecutive scoreless innings, the Giants tied it up in the seventh.

Irvin doubled off the left field wall, aided by Pafko's wide throw to second.

Lockman bunted in front of the plate and Irvin beat Walker's throw to third.

Thomson got a ball deep enough to center to let Irvin come home but Mays, the widely-touted rookie, again flivvered, hitting into a double play.

This state of affairs gave the Dodgers new life and they put the winning run on third in the eighth, with one gone, when Reese and Snider singled to right.

Reese scored and Snider went clear to third on a wild pitch with Robinson at the plate. With the count 3-1 on Robinson he was purposely passed.

Pafko was given a hit on a ball that squirted off Thomson's hands near the bag and Snider scored.

Cox shot a single through Thomson and Robinson raced home.

8
BOB GIBSON:
MR. COURAGEOUS

There's something besides ability which separates the superstar from the average baseball player. Courage and determination are other ingredients that help give the star his special glow. The team that has someone with an abundance of ability, courage and determination usually finds success a common partner. Here's a story about one of those athletes, on what was probably his greatest day.

The game described here in Mickey Herskowitz's story was one of seven straight won by

Gibson in World Series action. Each victory came in a complete game performance. With one other complete game in post-season play, Gibson owns the record for consecutive complete games. He won it as he lost a 4-1 pitching battle with Mickey Lolich in the seventh game of the 1968 Series. It was one of the few times Gibby failed to strike out 10 batters in a Series game—he holds the record with five such performances.

Bob Gibson was still showing his superstardom in 1973, when he suffered a serious leg injury at Shea Stadium, had surgery in August and came back to win a game on September 29 with his team fighting a losing battle for a championship.

By Mickey Herskowitz

Superpowered Bob Gibson won the most trumpeted pitchers' duel in World Series lore Wednesday, but it turned out to be against Sandy Koufax.

While his teammates took the menace out of Dennis McLain, Gibson struck out 17 flailing Tigers for a series record and fired the St. Louis Cardinals to a 4–0 victory in the opening of baseball's national test matches.

Gibson kept the suspense building in a game that was decided as early as the fourth inning, fashioning a performance that for sheer artistry and impact must stand with Don Larsen's perfect game.

The tall, liquid right-hander had a sellout crowd of 54,692 fans standing, screaming, and shuddering with joy as he struck out the side in the ninth to eclipse the record established by Koufax.

The retired Dodger left-hander had whiffed 15 New York Yankees in the 1963 classic, and Gibson entered the ninth needing one to tie.

He had been the entire show, a towering Shakespearean figure, since the fourth inning, when Mike Shannon's hit produced the only run he really needed, and Julian Javier singled across two more for comfort.

The crowd regarded Lou Brock's bases-empty homer in the seventh off Pat Dobson, the second of three Detroit pitchers, as merely a nice distraction.

So in the ninth it was Gibson against the Tigers, Koufax and the record book, and the crowd was hip. Even before the item appeared on the message board in center field, the fans knew that Robert Gibson, from the tall corn country of Nebraska, was pitching one for the ages.

Mickey Stanley, the transplanted shortstop, led off for Detroit, carried the count to 2–2, fouled off four pitches, and singled sharply to center, his second hit of the day.

But that merely heightened the drama, allowing Gibson to stretch the challenge, to achieve his record at the expense of Detroit's power . . . Kaline, Cash, and Horton. Power against Power. The perfect setting.

So here was Al Kaline, a beautiful player who had waited 16 years for this moment. Gibson struck him out with a fast ball low and away for No. 15. The record was tied. Sandy Koufax had company.

Now came Norm Cash, the slugging first baseman, a left-handed hitter. The count was 1–2 when Cash lifted a pop fly toward the Cardinal dugout, and as Tim McCarver chased it, the crowd recoiled in near horror. There were shouts of "No, no." The ball drifted into seats.

Cash swung and missed on a breaking pitch, and the fans leaped to their feet, as though someone had pressed a button that sent an electric charge through every seat. That was No. 16. Bob Gibson had struck out more batters in one game than any pitcher in World Series history.

The noise rose and swelled and swirled around the cantilevered rim of Busch Stadium, turning it into a whirlpool of sound.

McCarver, his catcher, stepped in front of home plate and grinned at Gibson, arms spread in a gesture that said, "Soak it up. It's all for you."

The intense, sometimes belligerent pitcher claimed later

to be unaware that he was on the verge of becoming immortal. "I didn't know what they were shouting about," he said, "until Tim stepped in front of the plate. Then I turned around and saw the scoreboard."

Did he recall what it said?

"Aw, I don't read that stuff," he protested. Then he added, "It said something about 16 strikeouts."

Number 17 was coming up next, in the blocky form of Willie Horton.

Horton took a lusty cut, as he always does, and missed on a slider, and Bob Gibson had struck out the side in the ninth inning, had finished it in a breezy, blazing sunburst of glory.

He had ventilated the opposition, reducing them to the status of paper Tigers. He struck out at least one in every inning, seven in the first three, and nailed Kaline and Cash each three times.

There really wasn't much else, but when you have Caruso you don't need juggling acts.

Gibson became the third pitcher ever to win six consecutive World Series, joining Lefty Gomez and Red Ruffing of the long-ago Yankees.

Thirteen of his 22 victories this season were shutouts, but none had been pitched under such pressure, in what had been advertised as a most personal duel.

And what of Denny McLain, Detroit's swashbuckling 31-game winner? His role in history was reduced to that of the fellow off whose head William Tell shot the apple.

The stocky right-hander was wild-high and unsteady and hung up on threes. He walked three, struck out three, allowed three hits and three runs.

His only moment of splendor occurred in the second inning, after McCarver tripled to right-center. Denny hitched up his belt, which incidentally, he wears alarmingly low, and struck out Shannon and Javier to end the threat.

An inning later Brock reached base on a fielder's choice, stole second as the crowd urged him on, and continued to third when catcher Bill Freehan's throw skipped into center field. But Curt Flood popped up to dispose of that problem.

In the fourth McLain walked himself into a jam from which the Tigers never emerged. Roger Maris went to first on four pitches, and after Orlando Cepeda lifted an infield pop, so did McCarver.

That brought manager Mayo Smith jogging out of the dugout to chat with McLain, who worried the dirt around the mound with his spikes as they consulted.

But words couldn't save them. Shannon rifled a single into left field, scoring Maris. McCarver hastened to third and Shannon moved to second when Horton overran the ball in left for an error.

On the first pitch to him, Javier laced a hit on the ground past Cash, two more runs sped home, and the Cardinals led, 3–0.

With McLain due up in the top of the sixth, Smith removed him for pinch hitter Tom Matchick, and Denny's World Series debut ended under a shower nozzle.

Pat Dobson relieved for Detroit and served up Brock's homer in the seventh, a golf shot that carried about 400 feet. Lou jammed a shoulder sliding back in the third, but it didn't appear to harm his swing.

Don McMahon, the antique of Detroit pitchers at 38, blanked the Cards in the eighth, but by then everyone was itching to see Gibson keep his date with the archives.

Only once had the Tigers threatened, in the sixth, the only inning in which Gibson allowed more than one hit. With one out Dick McAuliffe singled. Stanley struck out and then Kaline drilled a double to left, McAuliffe holding at third. A base hit here could have restored a sense of urgency to the contest, possibly.

But Cash struck out, and there it went.

The Cardinals collected six hits and stole three bases, flashing glimpses of their daring speed. Detroit touched Gibson for five hits and committed three errors, a somewhat shaggy effort by the American League champions.

If there was a bright spot for Detroit, it would be the play of Stanley, the outfielder turned shortstop, starting only his seventh game of a new position under the thickest of pressures.

He handled five chances cleanly, including the first ball batted by a Cardinal, a lead-off grounder by Brock. It was almost as though they planned it that way, reminding one of a sandlot game where someone says, "Hit it to Izzy, he can't catch it."

But Stanley proved himself, almost alone among the Tigers.

Gibson's line score, for strikeouts, looked like this: 2, 3, 2, 1, 1, 2, 2, 1, and 3. In the ninth a firecracker exploded with a large bang in the outfield, but no one flinched, so accustomed had the crowd grown to the sound of Bob's fast ball. He supported it with a curve and slider that kept the Tigers lunging.

So now the Tigers turn to lefty Mickey Lolich in the second game Thursday, against Nelson Briles, at least reasonably sure that the worst has already happened to them.

9
WILLIE MAYS:
TOUGH DECISION

Willie Mays began his great career playing with the New York Giants. He later was a superstar for the San Francisco Giants, but finished his career wearing the uniform of the New York Mets. Mays completed his playing days in the 1973 World Series at the Oakland Coliseum. The "Say Hey" kid loved to play baseball, so you can imagine how difficult it was for the veteran to say he'd prefer to be on the bench in the twilight of his career. The day after Mays gave the interview which produced this story by Ed Levitt, he had his final hit—a twelfth-inning single that drove in the go-ahead run and helped the Mets record a 10-7 triumph.

By Ed Levitt

Willie Mays saw it, heard it and loved it.

"All those 'Welcome to Oakland' signs and that big ovation when I was introduced, man, that gets to you. I don't care how long you been in this game, you feel it. I love the people here and the way they treat me. But I'd rather be booed and win than cheered and lose."

It was Willie, with a towel draped around him, sitting on a stool in the solemn Met clubhouse after the A's won the World Series opener and saying: "It's still exciting for me. Remember, I haven't been in a World Series since 1962. New York was in that one, too. Only that time it was the Yankees and I was with the Giants.

"These things are special. I got a kick out of the fans. I had the feeling they wanted me to get a hit. And when I did in the first inning, I heard people cheer.

"The discouraging thing is, we didn't win. But we've been down this road before. We lost the opening game of the playoffs and came back to win. We just need Rusty."

Mays was playing the outfield because Rusty Staub was out of the lineup with a sore right shoulder. He may play today.

"If Rusty is ready to play now, then I won't play," said Willie. "Rusty is 29, I'm 42. These young kids were the ones who put it all together. They got us in the World Series. They should be playing.

"During the season, I'd talk to the young players quite a bit. They don't need me to talk to them now. They know what it's all about. They know how to win.

"Sure, I'd like to finish my career by playing again in the Series, and I'm sure I'll get another shot.

"But I wouldn't do it if I thought the kids on the club resented it. I don't want them to feel I'm in it for my own glory. I don't need it. That's why I'd prefer Rusty play. And when he plays, I sit on the bench."

Willie was asked about his fielding error.

"I bobbled the ball but it didn't cost any runs," he said. "It's hard to play the outfield here. The grass is about two, three inches high. You don't know how the ball will bounce. It'll take me a few games to get used to it.

"You got to realize I haven't been playing lately. I hadn't played in a month and a half. You're not sharp when you lay off that long.

"That's why I'm hoping Rusty plays. He's seen a lot of action. He made that great catch in the playoffs, crashing against the wall. He's a big man on this club. We need him."

Willie was asked about Ken Holtzman, the A's winning pitcher yesterday.

"He was always tough against us when he played in the National League, but now he's changed a little. Winning all those games for the A's has given him more confidence. I think he's a better pitcher now. He sure throws a lot of fastballs.

"With both teams having such good pitching, I think there'll be more 2-1 games. We don't play any easy games. I understand the A's are the same way. That's why it'll be a good Series."

And Willie Mays summed up his World Series opener by insisting it was easier on him playing than watching.

"During the past month, when I wasn't playing, I lost six pounds," he said. "I was just worrying about the guys. This is a great bunch. I wanted these kids to win the pennant. Now I want them to win the World Series. But it's gonna be tough."

10
DON LARSEN:
ALL BY HIMSELF

There were more than 175 no-hit games pitched in major-league baseball from 1880 through 1974. Only one was accomplished in the spotlight of World Series competition. On October 8, 1956, Don Larsen wrote his name indelibly into the history of baseball as he pitched a perfect game, retiring all 27 batters he faced. Yogi Berra, who was catching for the Yankee right-hander, calls the game the most memorable of his lengthy career.

By Shirley Povich

The million-to-one shot came in. Hell froze over. A month of Sundays hit the calendar. Don Larsen today pitched a no-hit, no-run, no-man-reach-first game in a World Series.

On the mound at Yankee Stadium, the same guy who was knocked out in two innings by the Dodgers on Friday came up today with one for the record books, posting it there in solo grandeur as the only Perfect Game in World Series history.

With it, the Yankee right-hander shattered the Dodgers, 2-0, and beat Sam Maglie, while taking 64,519 suspense-limp fans into his act.

First there was mild speculation, then there was hope, then breaths were held in slackened jaws in the late innings as the big mob wondered if the big Yankee right-hander could bring off for them the most fabulous of all World Series games.

He did it, and the Yanks took the Series lead three games to two, to leave the Dodgers as thunderstruck as Larsen himself appeared to be at the finish of his feat.

Larsen whizzed a third strike past pinch-hitter Dale Mitchell in the ninth. That was all. It was over. Automatically, the massive 226-pounder from San Diego started walking from the mound toward the dugout, as pitchers are supposed to do at the finish.

But this time there was a woodenness in his steps and his stride was that of a man in a daze. The spell was broken for Larsen when Yogi Berra ran onto the infield to embrace him.

It was not Larsen jumping for joy. It was the more demonstrative Berra. His battery-mate leaped full tilt at the big guy. In self-defense, Larsen caught Berra in mid-air as one would catch a frolicking child, and that's how they made their way toward the Yankee bench, Larsen carrying Berra.

There wasn't a Brooklyn partisan left among the 64,519, it seemed, at the finish. Loyalties to the Dodgers evaporated in sheer enthrallment at the show big Larsen was giving them, for this was a day when the fans could boast that they were there.

So at the finish, Larsen had brought it off, and erected for himself a special throne in baseball's Hall of Fame, with the first Perfect Game pitched in major-league baseball since Charlie Robertson of the White Sox against Detroit 34 years ago.

But this was one more special. This one was in a World Series. Three times, pitchers had almost come through with no-hitters, and there were three one-hitters in the World Series books, but never a no-man-reach-base classic.

The tragic victim of it all, sitting on the Dodger bench, was sad Sal Maglie, himself a five-hit pitcher today in his bid for a second Series victory over the Yankees. He was out of the game, technically, but he was staying to see it out and it must have been in disbelief that he saw himself beaten by another guy's World Series no-hitter.

Mickey Mantle hit a home run today in the fourth inning and that was all the impetus the Yankees needed, but no game-winning home run ever wound up with such emphatic second-billing as Mantle's this afternoon.

It was an exciting wallop in the fourth inning only, because after that Larsen was the story today, and the dumfounded Dodgers could wonder how this same guy, who couldn't last out two innings in the second game, could master them so thoroughly today.

He did it with a tremendous assortment of pitches that seemed to have five forward speeds, including a slow one that ought to have been equipped with back-up lights.

Larsen had them in hand all day. He used only 97 pitches, not an abnormally low number because 11 pitches an inning is about normal for a good day's work. But he was the boss from the outset. Only against Pee Wee Reese in the first inning did he lapse to a three-ball count, and then he struck Reese out. No other Dodger was ever favored with more than two called balls by Umpire Babe Pinelli.

Behind him, his Yankee teammates made three spectacular fielding plays to put Larsen in the Hall of Fame. There was one in the second inning that calls for special description. In the fifth, Mickey Mantle ranged far back into left center to haul in Gil Hodges' long drive with a backhand shoetop grab that was a beaut. In the eighth the same Hodges made another bid to break it up, but Third Baseman Andy Carey speared his line drive.

Little did Larsen, the Yankees, the Dodgers, or anybody among the 64,519 in the stands suspect that when Jackie Robinson was robbed of a line drive hit in the second inning, the stage was being set for a Perfect Game.

Robinson murdered the ball so hard that Third Baseman Andy Carey barely had time to fling his glove upward in a desperate attempt to get the ball. He could only deflect it. But, luckily, Shortstop Gil McDougald was backing up, and able to grab the ball on one bounce. By a half-step, McDougald got Robinson at first base, and Larsen tonight can be grateful that it was not the younger, fleeter Robinson of a few years back but a heavy-legged, 40-year-old Jackie.

As the game wore on, Larsen lost the edge that gave him

five strikeouts in the first four innings, and added only two in the last five. He had opened up by slipping called third strikes past both Gilliam and Reese in the first inning.

Came the sixth, and he got Furillo and Campanella on pops, fanned Maglie. Gilliam, Reese, and Snider were easy in the seventh. Robinson tapped out, Hodges lined out, and Amoros flied out in the eighth. And now it was the ninth, and the big Scandinavian-American was going for the works with a calm that was exclusive with him.

Furillo gave him a bit of a battle, fouled off four pitches, then flied mildly to Bauer. He got two quick strikes on Campanella, got him on a slow roller to Martin.

Now it was the left-handed Dale Mitchell, pinch-hitting for Maglie.

Ball one came in high. Larsen got a called strike.

On the next pitch, Mitchell swung for strike two.

Then the last pitch of the game. Mitchell started to swing, but didn't go through with it.

But it made no difference because Umpire Pinelli was calling it Strike Number Three, and baseball history was being made.

Maglie himself was a magnificent figure out there all day, pitching hitless ball and leaving the Yankees a per-plexed gang, until suddenly, with two out in the fourth, Mickey Mantle, with two called strikes against him, lashed the next pitch on a line into the right-field seats to give the Yankees a 1-0 lead.

There was doubt about that Mantle homer because the ball was curving and would it stay fair? It did. In their own half of the inning, the Dodgers had no such luck. Duke Snider's drive into the same seats had curved foul by a few feet. The disgusted Snider eventually took a third strike.

The Dodgers were a luckless gang and Larsen a for-tunate fellow in the fifth. Like Mantle, Sandy Amoros lined one into the seats in right, and that one was a near thing for the Yankees. By what seemed only inches, it curved foul, the umpires ruled.

Going into the sixth, Marglie was pitching a one-hitter —Mantle's homer—and being outpitched. The old guy lost some of his stuff in the sixth, though, and the Yankees came up with their other run.

Carey led off with a single to center, and Larsen sacrificed him to second on a daring third-strike bunt. Hank Bauer got the run in with a single to left. There might have been a close play at the plate had Amoros come up with the ball cleanly, but he didn't and Carey scored unmolested.

Now there were Yanks still on first and third with only one out, but they could get no more. Hodges made a scintillating pickup of Mantle's smash, stepped on first and threw to home for a double play on Bauer who was trying to score. Bauer was trapped in a rundown and caught despite a low throw by Campanella that caused Robinson to fall into the dirt.

But the Yankees weren't needing any more runs for Larsen today. They didn't even need their second one, because they were getting a pitching job for the books this memorable day in baseball.

11
REGGIE JACKSON:
TIME FOR A SHOW

The New York Mets nearly won the 1973 World Series. But sometime between the fifth and sixth games, Reggie Jackson got his heart back into the competition. And the A's went on to retain their world championship with Jackson being named the Most Valuable Player. In the following story, Wells Twombly described the action as only he could.

By Wells Twombly

All morning long, the rain clouds arched their backs angrily over the world's grayest baseball stadium, getting ready to turn the infield into an alligator farm. Perhaps this was nature's way of telling Charlie Finley to slow down. Then, roughly an hour before game time, a patch of blue appeared, growing larger by the moment. Finally, the sun exploded, warming everything this side of the club owner's cold, cold heart. Clearly this was an omen.

Down in the Oakland A's dugout, certain glands were pumping away in the body of Reginald Martinez Jackson, home run hitter and resident phrase maker. After long, agonizing days of discomfort, this singular creature was about to join the World Series in progress. There probably isn't a better athlete in the American League than Jackson, a fact which he is just starting to recognize at age 27. Confidence could turn Reginald Martinez Jackson into a giant and he knows it.

"I think this is going to be my day," he informed a colleague. "I think it's my turn to do something. I've got this feeling."

For the first time since this vastly entertaining, but drastically unartistic, series began, people were talking about nothing but pure baseball. The owner wasn't threatening to fire anybody who dropped a pop foul and the manager hadn't quit to join the French Foreign Legion in days. There wasn't a touch of scandal anywhere. It was time to stop the nonsense and destroy the New York Metropolitans—an unworthy, but generally spirited team.

There are times when Jackson is a genuine, duly licensed team leader. There is a universality about the man, possibly because he transcends racial lines with black, white and Latin blood lines that tend to make him an everyman. He understands each of his teammates and they all find something in him they can identify. Reginald Martinez Jackson has soul, heart and machismo. Someday they're going to have to let him manage.

This was a desperate hour for the mad, mad, mad Oakland A's. They were down, three games to two, in a series with an obviously inferior baseball team. Trouble with the Metropolitans is that they don't realize they aren't very good. They play like champions and a club that doesn't know its own inferiority is a dangerous club indeed.

At last, Jackson has decided that winning the championship of the civilized world is a notable crusade. He came out of the Oakland dugout yesterday afternoon as the designated hero. In the first inning he discovered Joe Rudi on first base with one man out. He took one of Tom Seaver's fastballs and sent it bounding to the base of the wall in left field. One run scored.

Then, in the third, with two men out, Sal Bando singled and Jackson hit another double. Another man scored despite the fact that New York second baseman, Felix Milan, who's been playing this series like an elderly gentleman ready to go home for the winter hobbled Rusty Staub's poor throw in short right. There he was again in the eighth inning, singling to center and coasting all the way to third when Don Hahn, a San Francisco Giant dropout, let the ball dribble past him for a two-base error.

Up stepped Jesus Alou with a sacrifice fly to left that fetched Reginald home with the third and final run in a 3-1 Oakland victory that was undoubtedly the first truly decent game of the great Oktoberfest.

"All I wanted to do out there today was make catches, hit baseballs, slide and get my uniform dirty," said Jackson, who simply couldn't wait to talk to the press, now that he is convinced of his own ability to not only communicate, but to charm. "In order to play this game well there has to be a little bit of boy in you. That garbage in New York kind of took the boy out of me. It wasn't the World Series, it was something grim and awful. All I wanted to do was get this thing over."

It got so dark and dismal that Jackson asked to be traded to the New York Yankees, because that's where Oakland manager Dick Williams is supposed to be going as soon as the series ends and he lets Finley know he's gone. The word came booming back: under no circumstances would Reggie Jackson be traded to anyone. He could reasonably expect to outlast both Williams and Finley. Good grief, he was the Oakland franchise.

"He wouldn't talk to me. Then I discovered what he had on his mind. He let me know that I would die in green and gold. I'll go where the A's go—to Seattle or New Orleans or to Toronto or Europe. Maybe they'll stay in Oakland. That would be super with me."

For the first time since they discovered that there was such an event, the citizens of Oakland bought out every seat for a World Series game, which proves conclusively that the town is good for something else other than supporting the eastern end of the Bay Bridge.

"Maybe we've finally talked them into becoming baseball fans," said Jackson. "There were 49,333 people here today. I checked it out; this was the best crowd we ever had. They acted like they loved us and wanted us. Those people at Shea Stadium have encouraged the Mets to play better and the people here did the same thing for us. It was wonderful being back in the California sunshine."

Jackson approved of the way his friend James Augustus (Catfish) Hunter pitched, even though Williams had to rescue him before the game was over. In fact, Reggie hopes that Hunter gets $100,000 or more from Finley next year.

"I know I'll ask for it," said Catfish. "But I'm going to have to get to Finley before mah man Jackson does."

They make an interesting pair of spiritual leaders, Jackson the ghetto child from Philadelphia, and Hunter, the southern white child. In essence there isn't an ounce of difference between them. Heart and soul are the same qualities really.

"This meant a lot to me. I didn't play in the World Series last year and I cried at night a couple of times. I went to New York and they weren't talking about the great players in this series, guys like Catfish Hunter and Tom Seaver and Rusty Staub and Bud Harrelson and Bert Campaneris. They were talking about scandal. The talk about the batting cage was about what was going on in the clubhouse. Now we're back to baseball. Thank God."

Indeed that salvation of this gaudy, thoroughly weird event was the sixth game. It established the fact that when the Oakland A's face the New York Mets, it doesn't have to be an acid rock opera. It is entirely possible that baseball, in the classic sense, can be played. Trouble is that Charlie Finley loathes being upstaged. How can he take the play away from the final game? Well, he could dress himself in a saffron robe, shave his head, douse himself with gasoline . . . well, you know the rest.

12
RAY BOONE:
TOUGH ASSIGNMENT

Most of the stories in this book are about heroes. This one is about someone who failed to deliver in a clutch situation and that failure led to a defeat. Franklin Lewis says he wrote it to help encourage a youngster who followed Hall of Famer Lou Boudreau as shortstop of the Cleveland Indians. Certainly it took more than the story to keep Ray Boone in the majors. Still, the article may have helped. By the time Boone finished his career he had played 13 years as a major leaguer, compiled a respectable .275 lifetime batting average and collected 1,260 hits in 1,373 major-league games.

And Franklin Lewis had written a story that deserves to be remembered.

By Franklin Lewis

It's always so easy to write a story about a hero. You reach for the handiest superlatives, sprinkle them liberally with glory, and put into effect the thrilling achievements of the man honored. Sometimes a home run does the trick, sometimes a stiff right to the jaw, sometimes a 40-foot putt that trickles into the can on the 18th hole to end a bitter, tension-packed combat.

Well, this story won't be about a hero, and so maybe it will be a trifle difficult to put together. This is a piece about a young ball player, Ray Boone, who did nothing, and I'm not setting up the excuses in advance. The kid could have been a hero in the brightness of the first night of June. Oh, what a hero he could have been with 45,427 witnesses perched in the Stadium and with the prospect of a thousand headlines today to tell of a base hit or two that whipped the famous Boston Red Sox!

The kid didn't deliver the base hit. Fact is, he flopped twice when the bases were loaded, twice when there was one man on base. He even kicked a ground ball in the field. The boot didn't figure in the ball game, as it turned out, but there were some anxious moments.

And why, you may be asking, is it necessary or even timely to write a story about a youthful shortstop whose failures at the dish were strong contributing factors to the defeat of the Indians? Well, maybe this kind of a story will help Ray Boone. He can use some help. All young ball players can use a lift. A handy gadget, the pat on the back.

Besides, the kid is following a tough act. He's coming along after Louie Boudreau, the best shortstop of our times. If Boone were filling in for almost any other ball player in almost any other league or situation, there would be a limit to the significance attached to his sorrows with the stick. But people are sure to compare Boone to Boudreau, even as they were lining them up in their minds last night in the Stadium or in assorted parlors and television alleys.

I remember what Johnny Berardino said last summer when he played shortstop for a few games because Louie got himself bruised and battered in a collision at second base. Johnny had a spot of bad fortune with a few baseballs and the loyal loud louts in the seats inverted their cheers in honor of John.

"What do they want?" inquired the unhappy Berardino.

"I'm replacing the best shortstop in the business. Nothing I could do would be good enough."

Before Berardino could suffer too much, and before an accurate comparison of Louie and his understudy could be completed, the Boy Manager was back in the short field, somewhat the worse for a gimpy leg and a reversible thumb, but back just the same.

It is doubtful, for want of a better measurement, that any young player ever had more people giving him the telepathy than Boone got last night. As early as the second inning, with Larry Doby on first and one out, Ray had a chance to be a minor immortal. A home run, his first in the majors, would tie the score. Any base hit would help. But Ray flied out.

That was only the beginning. In the third, he was up with three on and two out, and by then one run would have tied the score. Here was certainly material for drama, a chance for the kid subbing for the king of shortstops to fill up his dream bowl for the year. Ray went to the full count, three-and-two. You squirmed in your seat, I imagine. I did. You were swinging the bat, too, on this next pitch. But Ray didn't swing. Mickey Harris, the lefty, shot a fast ball across knee-high. Ray passed a fleeting prayer for a base on balls, but he knew he was dead, even as Umpire Ed Hurley's right arm struck down the quota of bugs around home plate.

No hero yet was Ray Boone, but there were to be other opportunities. In the fifth he faced Harris for the third time and again there were three mates aboard. Maybe now there was a hint of a pinch hitter for the kid. As he kneeled in the batter's circle while Butch Keltner was luring a pass, Ray looked back toward the Cleveland bench two or three times, as if half expecting to see Louie Boudreau get to his feet and jiggle the ends of the bats in the rack.

Louie did get to his feet, but he only leaned out from under the dugout ledge and encouraged Boone with gestures and voice. Ray hit the second pitch, a towering foul in back of first base. Only one runner was on base in the seventh when, again with two out, the kid was the hitter.

He grounded snappily to short. A fifth attempt, in the ninth, was a liner to left center that Dominic DiMaggio, the Little Professor, gathered to his chest in a bucket catch after a hard sprint.

No, there would be no laurel for Ray's brow, just a memory of eight men that he left on the sacks. The number is included for accuracy and not for criticism.

Personally, I'm glad I wasn't in Ray Boone's shoes last evening, though I may have made up in wishful thinking what I lacked in physical replacement. I just thought I'd unwind a half yard of words that might let Ray know, as I'd want any young ball player to know, that the gents who write publicly of all these tribulations in baseball are not ogres with poison dripping from each fingertip.

Fundamentally, we're a sentimental lot. We're also spoiled by daily and annual visions of Louie Boudreau at short and at the plate. So there is no necessity for Boone to feel the heebies. Nobody's ever followed Louie yet. Besides, if some of the other guys had picked up a timely hit, things might have been better for Ray's side.

So it went, the story of a kid who wasn't a hero. Maybe he will be one soon.

13
THE 1949 YANKEES:
A TEAM OF DESTINY

Are injuries an acceptable excuse for failure to win a championship? Those who don't feel they are can always point to Casey Stengel's 1949 New York Yankees. Here's the climax to the story of the Yankees and their injuries that year, as told by Bob Stevens.

By Bob Stevens

Brooklyn, N.Y., October 8—At 5:08 this afternoon, the Team of Destiny moved forever into the hearts of baseball people the world over.

With floodlights shining on a World Series for the first time in history, a blazing fast ball crashed into the glove of Yogi Berra underneath the furiously slashing bat of Brooklyn's Gil Hodges, and the New York Yankees were champions of all baseball for the 12th time.

The Team of Destiny, they called it, a courageous gang of wired-together fighters who didn't know they were so physically battered that they weren't supposed to win. They didn't know, so they did win, sweeping virtually unchecked to victory in the 46th renewal of the World Series, four games to one.

The score here today in an Ebbets Field that is still looking for its first world champion was 10-6, the result of a relentless mid-game drive that was destined to stand up against the frantic challenges of a broken-hearted bunch of Bums from the banks of the Gowanus.

It was destined to stand for the Team of Destiny. Wracked by 71 major injuries, in charge of a "funny" man named Casey Stengel, and confronted with a situation in which they had to beat the power-laden Boston Red Sox on successive afternoons to win the American League pennant a week ago today, the Yankees did the impossible.

Probably never before in the history of the game have so many people cheered so deeply for the success of one aggregation of athletes. Only in Brooklyn had there been convictions of a contrary nature, but even here tonight voices are ringing out in praise of a ball club that outplayed and outfought the beloved Bums at every turn.

So, at 5:08, the incomparable Joe Page sent whirling to the plate the pitch that brought the Team of Destiny safely home, and left its foes lost and bewildered for the fifth time in World Series journeys. The Bums have yet to win the fall classic, have thrice been beaten off by the proud Yankees, starting in 1941, and it was the mighty Page, the same guy who closed shop for them in Yankee

Stadium in 1947, who dimmed the lights on Flatbush Avenue this time.

Page, called to the rescue of Vic Raschi, a battered figure in a perspiration-drenched uniform, faced only nine men during those last breathless innings. He struck out four of them, including three in the ninth.

It would be hard to forget the scene that took place down on the diamond when that last strike was thrust home. Weary and confused, Page didn't know what he had done. He started to walk off the hill, head down as though he had lost his last friend, and then came back into the roaring world. Berra slammed the ball at him, shouting and jumping, and waving his arms. It was then that Lefty Joe realized that everything for which he had labored so magnificently this year had been gained.

He caught the ball, staggered back a little, and then broke out on a dead run for a delirious Yankee locker room. Joe DiMaggio, who contributed a thunderous home run to the rout of the Bums today, called this team "the gamest, fightingest gang of guys that ever lived." Fighting gang, Team of Destiny, whatever they're called, in my mind they're New York Yankees. That name itself embraces all that is great in baseball.

The Dodgers, who were to be swept out of contention in five games, fought back desperately with six pitchers and four pinch-hitters, but couldn't overcome the lead the Yankees built by mid-game. It was 10–1 before the Bums came to the plate in the sixth and, even though they battered Raschi out of sight with four runs in that frame, it didn't seem important. There was always Joe Page, and the Bums got him.

As the result of the artistic hammering his Dodgers took, Manager Burt Shotton will be the target of more than a few questions as long as he lives. He let an obviously "off" Rex Barney suffer until the Yankees were in front, 5-0. Then he mysteriously permitted Pitcher Jack Banta to hit for himself after Roy Campanella had doubled in the third.

Either move, had it been made differently, might have sent the Series to six games. Neither was made, and the final coronation of the 1949 Yankees was that much more simple.

Barney wasn't long putting the Bums behind the count. He walked Phil Rizzuto and Tommy Henrich on nine pitches, struck out Berra, and worked the count to 3-2 on the great DiMaggio before Joe lined out to Duke Snider at the 393-foot mark in centerfield. Before Joe crashed that one, Barney had tried to pick Rizzuto off second and threw the ball into centerfield, advancing the runners. Snider did a beautiful job of robbing DiMag of a double or triple, but the blow still scored Rizzuto. Bobby Brown, another of the San Francisco boys who distinguished themselves today, singled through the box to drive in Henrich and the Yanks were out winging, 2-0.

Incidentally, this final game was pretty well dominated by kids from our side of the Nation. Brown collected two singles, a walk and a triple; Gene Woodling, who led the PCL in hitting with .385 as a Seal last year, bagged two doubles and a single; DiMag belted a home run, and Gerry Coleman gave a single and double to the cause. Verily, the San Francisco-New York Yankees beat the Bums today.

The embattled Barney escaped with his life in the second, but never saw the end of the third. When DiMaggio laced another screaming line drive into centerfield that Snider clawed sensationally off his shoe tops, Barney must have been frightened to death by the noise of the ball roaring over his head. He walked Brown, saw Woodling single, passed Cliff Mapes to load the bases, and then caved in all over when Coleman poked a ground single between short and third to score Bobby and Gene.

Shotton had enough, by then, and derricked Rex for Banta. Raschi immediately pounded a single off Jack, counting Mapes, and the Yankees were 5-0 on the good side.

The Dodgers scratched out a lonesome onesome in the third on Campanella's double and PeeWee Reese's single, but DiMaggio got that back in the fourth when he slugged a home run into the lower tier back of the left-field foul line. It was only his second hit of the Series, and Joe enjoyed to its fullest that wonderful trot around the bases.

Banta was battered for another New York tally in the fifth when Woodling plastered a double off the scoreboard, was bunted to third, and moved across on Coleman's grounder to Hodges at first. Gil momentarily fumbled the ball, allowing Woodling to come on in unchallenged.

Young Carl Erskine was buried in the Yankee sixth, another three-run frame that was reminiscent of the Yankees of old. Power, real hairy-chested, muscle-bulged power, was unleashed and the Bums cringed before it.

Rizzuto walked, and the spark was lit. Henrich swatted a single to left, and both he and Phil fidgeted on the base paths while Berra popped to left and DiMag skied to Jackie Robinson back of second. Then—whap!

Brown tripled off the right-field fence and Erskine, a family man with not too much life insurance, was yanked out of there, to be replaced by Joe Hatten. Joe was of no immediate good. Woodling placed a line drive double between left and center and the Team of Destiny had all the runs it was to get, and three more than it was to require.

The Bums came to life again in the home half of the sixth, scoring on a double by Snider and a sharp single to right by Gene Hermanski. The Bums then pounded the arm-weary Raschi off the premises in the seventh with a four-run display that caused vocal commotion, but nothing more substantial than that.

After Reese went out, Spider Jorgensen walked, Snider singled him to third, and Robinson brought him across on a deep fly to Woodling in left. Hermanski walked on four pitched balls, and Hodges, after taking a ball and then a called strike, tied into a fast ball and drove it 18 rows into the left-field bleachers.

It also drove Mr. Raschi out of sight, and brought upon the scene Mr. Page, who required only three cracking fastballs to dispose of Pinch-hitter Luis Olmo and retire the side.

When Bruce Edwards singled for Erv Palica in the eighth, and Page personally started the rally-murdering double play by fielding Reese's grounder and whipping it to Rizzuto, the majority of the 33,711 in attendance arose and filed silently toward the exits.

Lefty Joe was in slight trouble in the ninth when Eddie Miksis led off with a double. But Page struck out Snider, gave the same business to Robinson, walked Hermanski and then poured the coal to Hodges, who had homered in the seventh to fan life into the fading Bums. He also fanned all the life out of them in the ninth, and for keeps.

There will be no game tomorrow. The Team of Destiny, victors in six of its last seven starts, games that first gave it the flag, then the world championship, has placed the final period at the end of one of the greatest stories baseball has ever told.

Sitting back relaxed tonight is the one-time "clown" who, until a few months ago, was never taken seriously as a baseball brain, the man who directed the impossible, Manager "Ole Case" Stengel of the Yanks.

14
THE WHIZ KIDS: MORE DODGER FRUSTRATION

Definitions of the verb "excite" include: (a) to call to activity, (b) to rouse feeling. A synonym of the word is "provoke." Certainly that's what the Brooklyn Dodgers did for their fans even though the team won only one World Series from 1900 until it moved to California after the 1957 season. Elsewhere in this book is the story of the wild finish experienced by Brooklyn fans in 1951. Here's the game that made the Brooklyn fans start talking about 1951.

Bob Stevens' last-paragraph prediction was correct. The Yankees swept the Phillies in four straight games, and somehow the Whiz Kids

aged quickly. In 1951 the Phillies finished fifth
in the National League. They have been strug-
gling unsuccessfully ever since to produce another league championship.

By Bob Stevens

Brooklyn, Oct. 1—The agonizing growing pains that
were felt around the world were finally ended here today,
and the patient is delirious. The Philadelphia Phillies, the
incredible Whiz Kids, today became of age.

After a tortuous, pain-wracked, blood-letting final two
weeks of a National League stretch run that will never, no
never, be forgotten, the beardless wonders of Eddie Saw-
yer tacked the Phillies' first pennant to the mast in 35
years by prevailing over the Brooklyn Dodgers, 4-1, in ten
innings.

It wasn't an ordinary game of baseball. It was terrific.
Heart hurting and indescribably dramatic. It was youth,
kid stuff, against a tooled, especially selected group of
veterans from the Nation's greatest farming system that
came out on top in a grim, last-game struggle for the pennant.

It left 35,073 people, jam-packed in this house of heroics, blunders and histrionics, limp with emotions, some
sad, some maniacal as the loved and sentimentally favored
Whiz Kids grew up.

And, it was done in manly fashion, muscularly, dramati-
cally, conclusively.

With one away, runners on first and second, and the
count against him, two and one, Dick Sisler, whose pappy,
George, was the greatest first baseman of his day, became,
at least for a fleeting, monumental moment, his equal by
smashing his 13th home run into the left-field bleachers.
It wound up 35 years of desperate building, 35 years of
being ridiculed throughout the National League as the set-
ups of all time, 35 years of fanciful dreaming.

They're toasting Sisler and the cherubic-faced Robin Roberts, one day into his 25th year, tonight throughout a Nation that takes its baseball more seriously than its politics.

Sisler delivered the coup de grace, a fancy way of saying the blow that killed father and stilled the waters of the Gowanus and ended one of the most courageous uphill struggles in baseball history. From nine games off the pace on September 12, the doughty, unbelievably audacious Dodgers cut steadily into the lead of the faltering, choking, stumbling Phils to come within one game, one pitch, actually, of forcing a play-off.

They didn't get it. Sisler and Roberts saw to that.

The drama, and it dripped, was crowded into the last of the ninth, when a colossal blunder wiped the Bums out of contention as surely as though they refused to take the field, and the top of the tenth, the pay-off panel.

But, let's crown the kids with the laurels of conquest, before hacking away at the disconsolate Dodgers who lost behind their 19-game winner, massive Don Newcombe.

Roberts, who becomes a 20-gamer today, opened the tenth with a single through the box and into center. Newcombe furiously pounded his glove in vexation, and Ralph Branca continued his frantic warming-up in the Bums' bull pen. Then, Eddie Waitkus, the narrow survivor of a lovesick babe's bullet, looped a single to the feet of the diving Duke Snider and the kids started filing for scoring privileges.

Ritchie Ashburn, who had his moment in this great hour of Philadelphia triumph, tried to bunt the boys along, but Newcombe swallowed his grounder and fired to Billy Cox at third to nail Roberts, who came in on a wing, a prayer and a cloud of dust.

Newcombe, momentarily reprieved, breezed two strikes past the eager Sisler and the few Phils partisans who dared open their yaps in this land of Bum lovers, groaned audibly, and miserably. A ball, high, which Sisler started after, then reconsidered, thudded into Catcher Roy Campanella's moist glove.

Six thousand dollars' worth of pitch was delivered then

by the sweat-drenched Newcombe. It was a little high, a little on the far-away corner, and Sisler lashed out. The ball was met squarely, and the crowd hushed as it started its epic flight into left field. Cal Abrams backed into the wall, groping, clutching, jumping, impatiently, pitifully. Into the stands it disappeared, and Ebbets Field exploded. So did Philadelphia. And, so did Sisler.

Losing his dignity, Dick pogo-sticked down the line from first to second, waving his arms and screaming.

He rounded third base to cheers he'd never before heard, fell into the arms of his teammates at the plate, and went toward the dugout, there to shake hands and wink mischievously at his father, the great George of yesteryear.

Pappy didn't know whether to laugh or to cry. His son was a hero, but he got that way by beating Pappy's ball club, the Dodgers, for whom the elder Sisler works as a scout.

It was ironical, too, in another way. Accepted as the greatest first-baseman the game has ever known, George Sisler never made a World Series. Dick, the most successful son of an immortal in the business today, enters his second fall classic Wednesday when the New York Yankees rumble into Shibe Park. Dick first made it with the victorious St. Louis Cardinals in 1946.

After that blow the rest was anti-climactic. Roberts, now assured, poured the coal to Campanella and Pinch-hitters Jim Russell and Tommy Brown, and the growing pains were over. Win or lose to the Yankees, the Whiz Kids are men!

Brooklyn could have forced the issue into a three-game play-off except for an ill-advised play by third-base Coach Milt Stock in the ninth, Roberts' worst, and near fatal frame. After Abrams walked, Pee Wee Reese, who collected three of the five hits off Roberts, including a home run for the Bums' only score, singled. Snider then slashed a scorcher into center, and Abrams was off and running.

Instead of holding at third Cal was waved on in and a perfect throw from Ashburn to Catcher Stan Lopata cut down Abrams without a slide. It would have been the winning tally. Had Stock held Abrams at third, the bases would have been loaded, none out, and all the Dodgers needed then was a fly to the outfield to cinch their eleventh consecutive victory in a breath-taking stretch drive.

As it was, it left first base open, and Jackie Robinson was deliberately walked, rejamming the paths. Carl Furillo fouled out limply to Waitkus close to the box seats back of first, and Gil Hodges lofted a routine fly to Del Ennis in right to close out the inning.

It closed out the Dodgers, 1950 vintage, too. And ended in failure a comeback that would have rivaled the incredible move from last to first by the Boston Braves of 1914 after July 4.

Both the Phils' and the Dodgers' only runs were tinged with cheapness. In the sixth, the kids broke out into a 1-0 lead when, after two were down, Sisler singled, and Ennis dittoed. Del's blow was a broken back liner into short center that fell in a human puddle formed by Snider, Robinson and Furillo. Puddin'-head Jones then slashed a nifty through the box past Newcombe to tally Sisler.

In the bottom of the sixth, the Bums came back. Reese leaned into an outside curve and swept it high into right field. The ball thudded against the screen, bounced down onto the signboards, teetered precariously on the ledge, and finally lodged there while Ennis insanely jumped up and down waiting for it to come down.

Ordinarily it would have rolled off and been nothing more damaging than a double. But, in Ebbets Field, they don't do things in routine fashion. That I know from past experiences in this madhouse of bat and ball.

The Phils offered a mild protest, but were overruled and that freak blow, poorly hit, but expertly placed, loomed larger and larger as this pennant battle progressed. In finale, it meant nothing more than the run that deprived Roberts, truly a great pitcher with courage to spare, of a shutout.

For those who see their baseball in the dimensions of Seals Stadium back home, Joe Grace would have had to come in to latch on to Reese's homer, and Sisler's would have landed just about where Brooks Holder tends bar every night.

There was a difference, however. Sisler's clout meant $6000 to his mates. Which is an important piece of meaning.

Though a tense duel, it had its comedy, too. It happened in the seventh, and helped to momentarily relieve the tension that was mounting with each pitch. Hodges fouled back of the plate and down toward first base where Andy Seminick and Waitkus gave chase. Both tumbled into the laps of spectators, Waitkus' glove hitting in the middle of a beer cup and spraying everybody with wet suds, the greatest bath New York has seen since Anna Held jumped into a milk tub for Flo Ziegfeld to astonish, as well as tease, Broadway. Eddie wiped the foam off his mouth, smacked his lips, winked, and went back to work.

The kids, now the men, hustle back to Philly tonight while the Yankees, who will probably eat them alive, return to New York from Boston, where they will work out tomorrow in The House That Ruth Built.

15
ERNIE BANKS:
A BEAUTIFUL MAN

The world would be a lot better off if it were dominated by people like Ernie Banks. The former star of the Chicago Cubs was never too busy to greet people with a smile. He didn't complain about extra-inning games or double-headers. One of his favorite comments was, "It's a beautiful day, let's play three." Baseball would have little difficulty drawing fans if it could find the mold which developed Banks and put one of him on each team.

Banks continued to play with the Cubs through 1971. He had one major disappointment in his career. He never got to play in a World Series, because the Cubs never won a league championship.

By Stan Hochman

You turn a light bulb on 1,112 times and it's gonna
sputter, or go dim, or turn gray and useless on you.

They don't make tungsten filaments to match the fire
that burns inside Ernie Banks.

Banks has a handsome, gentle face and he blinks his
eyes in surprise when you tell him there must have been
September afternoons when buttoning on a Chicago uniform was painful drudgery.

"There are times," he confessed almost guiltily, "when I
start out for the ballpark and I don't have any zip. But
then I get out here, and something changes, something
happens."

This was yesterday, in the swish-swash silence of the
training room, before Banks went out to play leftfield after
1,061 games at shortstop and 50 more in an awkward
third-base experiment in 1957.

He is too naive to know that the Cubs are making him
the scapegoat of their own stupid deals, that they are
blaming him for a barren farm system and the inadequacy
of the other players in their daytime masquerade as big
leaguers.

"The management team talked to me about playing
leftfield," he said softly. "I asked them if they thought I
would be helping the club out there and they said yes."

Today, when he reads in the Chicago papers that
Vedie Himsl said, "Ernie came to us, it was his idea,"
Banks will nod and tell himself, "Yes, maybe that is the
way it really happened."

The Phillies' Tony Taylor was lumpy clay of a second
baseman when he broke in alongside Banks. He mourned
this frantic move, and the words came like tear drops:
"Banks is a great shortstop . . . he plays the hitters and
he plays the count . . . maybe he don't make spectacular
plays, but he makes all the plays. . . . They say he don't
make the doubleplay. One year we make hundred-and-

something doubleplays and the next year we second in the league."

Banks is realistic only about the limits of his range, the grace of his doubleplay moves. "I tried to know the pitching staff," he explains. "I tried to know the hitters and where they are apt to hit the ball. I practiced the doubleplay with the second baseman as much as I could, learning his moves."

Now they have forgotten that he set a National League record for fielding and that last year he made the fewest errors of any regular shortstop. And he played every game and he hit 40 homers every season.

"I always have the feeling that the next day I'm gonna do better," Banks said, walking eagerly out into the brittle sunshine of Wrigley Field.

He looked out at the pennants clacking in the wind alongside the scoreboard. "Night games, night games, night games," he laughed. "We will be home playing with the kids, when they're just starting in."

It is a bullfighter's gesture, to study the wind, to make smalltalk. In leftfield waited the horned menace of uncertainty, the ivy-camouflaged danger of the brick wall.

"I feel fine, just like starting a new job," he said. "I know I'm going to have to buckle down and practice. I don't want to embarrass myself or the fans who follow us."

He caught three fly balls, softened by the wind that blew at his back. He fielded one single, erect, like an infielder instead of in the cautious crouch of the outfielder.

"All you have to do is think about hitting out there," Hinsl had said earlier, in his clumsy explanation of the move.

"I looked at the dugout and at (George) Altman, and even at the stands for help on where to play hitters," Banks admitted afterwards.

"I started after every ball hit to the infield. I'm going to have to keep thinking where I must throw the ball in certain situations."

The Cubs have never finished in the first division in

Banks' seven seasons with them, but he never belittles his teammates or the other inhabitants of despair.

Yesterday, his code shattered in the hectic business of the switch to leftfield. His eyes twinkled and he lowered his voice. "Maybe it was a good break for me to break in against the Phillies. After that I didn't have to challenge any of the walls."

16
ROSE, HICKMAN, MORGANNA, AND NIXON

All-Star games frequently are nothing more than boring, with baseball's top performers just going out for some exercise. But Joe Gergen doesn't know how to write a boring baseball story.

What has happened to the characters who starred that day? Pete Rose, or "Charlie Hustle" as he's often called, still doesn't know how to relax in a baseball uniform. Ray Fosse didn't miss a game because of his collision with Rose, but a severely bruised shoulder hampered his swing and he never hit as well as he did before the injury. Jim Hickman never played in another All-Star Game. Morganna Roberts apparently gave up running onto the field to kiss players and gain publicity for her go-go dancing.

And Richard Nixon became interested in other things.

By Joe Gergen

It began with Richard Nixon and ended with Jim Hickman. Imagine. It began with red, white and blue bases and

---

ended in a black and blue collision. Imagine. It began with Morganna Roberts failing for the first time and ended with the American League failing for the eighth consecutive time. No imagination necessary.

The All-Star Game played last night in Cincinnati's Riverfront Stadium, a ball park of tomorrow because it isn't finished today, was an All-Star Game for all seasons. The President of the United States and Cincinnati threw out the first ball and waited 12 innings to see Hickman, another former loser, get a winning hit. Hickman, who still can't win them all, didn't get kissed by Morganna. Instead, he was hugged by Luman Harris. At least he didn't get hurt.

Dennis Menke left the park with a deep red spot on his cheek from a throw and a puffy bruise on his hand from a pitch, and Pete Rose needed an ice pack for his left knee. And they were the winners. Ray Fosse, one of the losers, looked so bad, he was sent to the hospital. And to think they call this an exhibition game. "It was fun," Bud Harrelson of the Mets said. "It was really fun."

The final score of the fun was National League, 5; American League, 4. The ending was the same, only different. The National League almost always wins, but they usually don't have to come from behind. Last night, they had to score three runs in the ninth and one in the 12th. And Rose had to run over Fosse at home plate. "Quite a collision," Gil Hodges, the manager, said. "It took a bulldog like Pete to score."

The game was strictly no contest for eight innings. Morganna had caused the only excitement until then by climbing out of the stands behind third base in the first inning and being pinched, literally, by a cop. She was dressed like Myra Breckenridge, trying to hide her sex and identity in a loose green top and brown slacks. She didn't fool Fritz Peterson, standing nearby in the American League dugout, the park policeman or anyone else in the stadium. "The cop had a real good hold on her," Peterson said. "When she was being led off, she said something into the dugout. I think it was, 'You can't win them all.' No, I remember now it was, 'Better luck next time.'"

Morganna, her baseball record now 5–1, was booked and released on $50 bail. "The first tape-measure job in Riverfront Stadium," a man commented.

Baseball had been saved from Morganna by an alert cop. But, by the ninth inning, it appeared nothing could save baseball from boredom. The American League had scored four runs without much fuss, the National League had scored one on a double-play grounder, Carl Yastrzemski was already being congratulated for winning the Most Valuable Player award, and the President was three outs from Washington. The American League, imagine, was going to win an All-Star Game.

Then Catfish Hunter of Oakland walked in from the bullpen. The first batter was Dick Dietz of the Giants, who had never swung a bat in an All-Star Game. He hit a very long home run over the center-field fence. "The second tape-measure job in Riverfront Stadium," the man said. Harrelson singled for his second single. One out later, Joe Morgan singled and the pitcher suddenly was Peterson. The batter, Willie McCovey, hit a grounder. "I thought it was a double play," Peterson said. It was a single, an AstroTurf single. The score was 4–3, the next pitcher, Mel Stottlemyre.

Roberto Clemente, who didn't want to come all the way to Cincinnati to play in an exhibition game, hit a long sacrifice fly and the game was tied. American League manager Earl Weaver thought about having a relief pitcher, a Ron Perranoski or a Lindy McDaniel, in that inning. He thought, Who needs them? That's what he said he thought. "What you're trying to get me to say is that I should take one pitcher off and put another on," he said, "and I'm not going to say that."

The 10th passed quickly, the 11th also, and the 12th was in danger of extinction. Yastrzemski had a soft hit, tying him with Ducky Medwick and Ted Williams for an All-Star record, in the top of the inning and the AL had nothing else. The NL had two quick outs before Rose hit a single off Clyde Wright. Then Billy Grabarkewitz singled and the batter was, of all people, Hickman.

That's the same Hickman of whom Casey Stengel once

sang, "You can't improve your average with your bat upon your shoulder, tra-la, tra-la, tra-la." The same Jim Hickman who it was said didn't need a bat to play the game. The same Jim Hickman who didn't get to last night's game until 5:00 P.M., who didn't get onto the field until the last National Leaguer was walking out of the batting cage, who was on two flights with mechanical difficulties on the same day in Chicago. In short, the same Jim Hickman.

Jim Hickman swung, the ball went into center field toward another former Met, Amos Otis, and Rose tore around third. Hickman ran into a bear hug from first-base coach Harris. Fosse, the catcher whom Rose had invited to his house for a bull session the previous night, stood waiting for the throw. He never got to catch it. Rose plowed into and over him, and Fosse rolled over in pain.

"He could have slid around him," Wright charged angrily. Rose, who got a bruised knee for his trouble, thought otherwise. "He was two or three feet up the line and straddling it," Rose said. "I started to slide and realized I couldn't make it to the plate that way. I play to win, so that's the way I had to play tonight. I know Frank Robinson would have done it, and that's the best player in their league.

"Besides," he said, leaning back on the training table, "it was Wright's fault. He threw the pitch to Hickman."

And so, Jim Hickman became an authentic American hero. "The biggest hit of my career," he said. And the American League had lost another one. "I'm 0-and-7 now," said Yastrzemski, looking suspiciously at his MVP trophy.

Morganna was dancing in Newport, Kentucky, when the President finally left for Washington.

17
BASEBALL
MOVES WEST:
AN ACT OF TREASON?

To boys who grew up in Brooklyn during
the 1950's, "Walter O'Malley" is a dirty word.
O'Malley has drawn well in Los Angeles, but
wouldn't Horace Stoneham love to have his
Giants calling Shea Stadium home? In 1957,
veteran baseball writer Dick Young provided
readers with a colorful, accurate, historical look
at the events that retired the main playing sites
of many of the game's immortals. Young, who
is one of the best known baseball writers of
modern times, leaves no doubt about his feelings and those of other devoted Dodger fans
who suffered and waited patiently for a championship team only to see it snatched from
them.

By Dick Young

This is called an obit, which is short for obituary. An
obit tells of a person who has died, how he lived, and
those who live after him. This is the obit on the Brooklyn
Dodgers.

Preliminary diagnosis indicates that the cause of death
was an acute case of greed, followed by severe political
complications. Just a year ago, the Brooklyn ball club
appeared extremely healthy. It had made almost a half-
million dollars for the fiscal period, more than any other
big-league club. Its president, Walter O'Malley, boasted

that all debts had been cleared, and that the club was in the most solvent condition of its life, with real-estate assets of about $5 million.

O'Malley contends that unhealthy environment, not greed, led to the demise of the Dodgers in Brooklyn. He points out that he became aware of this condition as long ago as 1947, when he began looking around for a new park to replace Ebbets Field, capacity 32,000.

At first, O'Malley believed the old plant could be remodeled, or at least torn down and replaced at the same site. But, after consultation with such a prominent architect as Norman Bel Geddes, and the perusal of numerous blueprints and plans, O'Malley ruled out such a possibility as unfeasible.

So O'Malley looked around for a new lot where he could build this bright, new, salubrious dwelling for his Dodgers; a dream house, complete with plastic dome so that games could be played in spite of foul weather, a plant that could be put to year-round use, for off-season sports and various attractions.

O'Malley suggested to the City of New York that the site of the new Brooklyn Civic Center, right outside the Dodger office windows in Boro Hall, would be ideal for the inclusion of a 50,000-seat stadium—a War Memorial stadium, he proposed.

That was very patriotic, the City Planning Commission said, but not a stadium; not there. Sorry.

So O'Malley looked farther, and hit upon the area at Flatbush and Atlantic Avenues—virtually the heart of downtown Brooklyn, where all transit systems intersect, and where the tired Long Island Railroad limps in at its leisure. O'Malley learned that a vast portion of the neighborhood, which included the congested Fort Greene market, had been declared a "blighted area" by city planners who had earmarked it for rehabilitation.

Here began one of the most forceful political manipulations in the history of our politically manipulated little town. With O'Malley as the guiding spirit, plans for establishment of a Sports Authority were born. It would be the work of such an Authority to issue bonds and build a stadium with private capital—utilizing the city's condemnation powers to obtain the land.

With O'Malley pushing the issue through his lifelong political contacts, the bill was drafted in Albany, passed overwhelmingly by the City Council, squeezed through the State Legislature by one vote, and ultimately signed into law by Governor Harriman.

At that moment, April 21, 1956, the prospects for a new stadium and a continuance of Brooklyn baseball were at their highest. Thereafter, everything went downhill. City officials, who had supported the bill originally, in the belief Albany would defeat it, went to work with their subtle sabotage. Appropriations for surveys by the Sports Center Authority were cut to the bone, and O'Malley shook his head knowingly. He was getting the works.

O'Malley, meanwhile, had been engaging in some strange movements of his own. He had leased Roosevelt Stadium, Jersey City, for three years with the announced intention of playing seven or eight games a season there. Later, he sold Ebbets Field for $3,000,000 on a lease-back deal with Marv Kratter. The lease made it possible for O'Malley to remain in Brooklyn, in a pinch, for five years. He had no intention of doing so—it was just insurance against things blowing up at both political ends.

Why was Ebbets Field sold?

Politicians claimed it was an O'Malley squeeze on them. O'Malley claimed it was a manifestation of his good intentions; that he was converting the club's assets into cash so that he might buy Sports Authority bonds and help make the new stadium a reality.

Then, O'Malley moved in a manner that indicated he didn't believe himself. At the start of '57 he visited Los Angeles. Two months later he announced the purchase of Wrigley Field. Shortly thereafter, Los Angeles officials, headed by Mayor Paulson and County Supervisor Ken Hahn, visited O'Malley at Vero Beach, Florida.

It was there, on March 7, that serious consideration of a move to Los Angeles crystallized in the O'Malley mind. He made grandiose stipulations to the L.A. authorities—and was amazed to hear them say: "We will do it."

From then on, Los Angeles officials bore down hard on the project, while New York's officials quibbled, mouthed sweet nothings, and tried to place the blame elsewhere. With each passing week, it became increasingly apparent the Dodgers were headed West—and, in an election year, the politicians wanted no part of the hot potato.

Bob Moses, park commissioner, made one strong stab for New York. He offered the Dodgers park department land at Flushing Meadow—with a string or two. It wasn't a bad offer—but not as good as L.A.'s.

By now, O'Malley's every move was aimed at the coast. He brought Frisco Mayor George Christopher to dovetail the Giant move to the coast with his own. He, and Stoneham, received permission from the NL owners to transfer franchises.

That was May 28—and since then, O'Malley has toyed with New York authorities, seeming to derive immense satisfaction from seeing them sweat unnecessarily. He was repaying them.

Right to the end, O'Malley wouldn't give a flat, "Yes, I'm moving"—as Stoneham had done. O'Malley was using New York as his saver—using it to drive a harder bargain with L.A.'s negotiator Harold McClellan, and using it in the event the L.A. city council were to reject the proposition at the last minute.

But L.A., with its mayor whipping the votes into line the way a mayor is expected to, passed the bill—and O'Malley graciously accepted the 300 acres of downtown Los Angeles, whereupon he will graciously build a ball park covering 12 acres.

And the Brooklyn Dodgers dies—the healthiest corpse in sports history. Surviving are millions of fans, and their memories.

The memories of a rich and rollicking history—dating back to Ned Hanlon, the first manager, and skipping delightfully through such characters as Uncle Wilbert Robinson, Casey Stengel, Burleigh Grimes, Leo Durocher, Burt Shotton, Charley Dressen, and now Walt Alston. The noisy ones, the demonstrative ones, the shrewd and cagey ones, and the confused ones. They came and they went but always the incredible happenings remained, the retold screwy stories, the laughs, the snafued games, the laughs, the disappointments, the fights, and the laughs.

And the players: the great ones—Nap Rucker, Zack Wheat, Dazzy Vance, Babe Herman, Dolph Camilli, Whit Wyatt, Dixie Walker; the almost great ones but never quite —like Van Lingle Mungo and Pete Reiser; the modern men who made up the Dodgers' golden era—Duke Snider, Preacher Roe, Hugh Casey—and the man who made history, Jackie Robinson, and the boy who pitched Brooklyn to its only world championship in 1955, Johnny Podres.

And the brass: the conflicts of the brothers McKeever, and the trials of Charley Ebbets; the genuine sentimentality of Dearie Mulvey and the pride of her husband, Jim Mulvey; the explosive achievement of Larry MacPhail; the unpopular but undeniable success of Branch Rickey—and now, Walter O'Malley, who leaves Brooklyn a rich man and a despised man.

18
TED WILLIAMS:
NO MIDDLE GROUND

It doesn't take a lot of words to make a well-written article. Evidence of this is the following story by Whitney Martin, who wrote this piece on Hall of Famer Ted Williams while working for The Associated Press.

By Whitney Martin

He's been castigated, maligned, insulted, traduced and caluminated.

He's been booed, hooted, jeered, derided, mocked, and scorned.

Yet when it dawned on the fans who were making a career of abusing Ted Williams that they probably were seeing him for the last time in a Red Sox uniform they suddenly discovered they loved the guy.

The very things about him they so loudly and caustically had criticized abruptly became endearing and admirable character traits.

If he didn't tip his cap after hitting a home run, so what? A man of his acknowledged genius as a slugger was entitled to his eccentricities, wasn't he? And what is wrong about a lode of stubborn independence running through such a vibrant, intense personality?

There never was anything static about the fans' reaction to the big guy. They either were for him with a fierce, unswerving loyalty, or their comments concerning him were splashed with vitriol. There just was no middle ground.

His mere appearance in the batting cage before a game brought a swelling roar from the crowd; the roar an admixture of cheers and boos. There always was a tense, electric expectancy that couldn't be hidden by the din when he approached the plate in a game, his long, loose frame jiggling like a puppet on strings, his every move a picture of eagerness and serious energy.

They came to boo him and to cheer him, and even those who booed him by their very outburst showed a grudging admiration. Their crudely expressed criticism was high praise indeed.

Touched almost beyond words by the whole-hearted tribute paid him on his final appearance at Fenway Park, responding graciously to the acclaim, he nevertheless remained in character to the last.

The character of a stubborn, independent, often contrary but never pallid individualist. He refused to doff his cap after rapping out a game-winning home run; a home run which seemed destined as a fitting climax of the great career of one of the game's most controversial figures.

Somehow it seemed fitting that he should ignore the

applause. He was Ted Williams, the Ted Williams the fans had come to love, even in secret. He would not have been Ted Williams if he had tipped his cap.

They have judged him only by what they have seen of him over the years, and read about him. The real Ted Williams has been hidden behind a mask of professed indifference to public opinion; a mask consciously donned to hide a kindness and generosity which he felt might be taken as a bid for sympathy, or the grandiose gesture of the showoff.

They didn't know of his secret visits to children's hospitals; of how he would load magazines in his car under cover of night and drop them anonymously on the steps of institutions where they would be most appreciated.

They didn't know about his own little farewell party, and how he invited each of the 35 guests personally, by telephone. And that the guests weren't club officials, or civic leaders, or men of high estate, but were ex-bat boys, and hotel clerks, and bell boys, and soda jerks.

In short, his friends who were such not because he was Ted Williams, the celebrity, but because he was Ted Williams, period.

There is a certain touching humility about that picture. The fans at Fenway Park must have sensed that humility in their final tribute to a great athlete.

19
MICKEY MANTLE: IT'S ALL OVER

How difficult is it to be a major league player? The hours are short and the pay is good. But it isn't all fun and games, as George Vecsey's story proves. Mantle earned his way into the Hall of Fame. It took some bats, some gloves, quick reaction—plus a lot of ability and heart. His name ranks high among all-time Yankees in many offensive categories, and he was probably the most powerful switch-hitter in the game of baseball. His .298 lifetime batting average is misleadingly low. It would have been much higher had it not been for injuries and decisions to prolong his career.

By George Vecsey

The retirement of a player as great as Mickey Mantle should inspire only a recitation of great deeds and enjoyable moments, yet his story must include frustration and unfulfillment along with the glory. Mantle never enjoyed his 18 years in New York the way many other stars have enjoyed their careers, and injuries and personal struggles were equally responsible.

For many years he seemed on the verge of becoming a happy, healthy star—he was certainly a hero to millions of fans—but injuries and temper delayed that process. Then in the closing years, after he had achieved many great things on the field and developed a relative maturity to appreciate them, he was cheered every time he poked his head out of the dugout.

However, Mantle understood that the cheers were for him as a descending star and he had never wished to be the central figure in a tragic-opera situation. When fans in Houston gave him a standing ovation last summer after he had struck out in the All-Star Game, he talked of being "tired" and retiring. The one glorious year of being whole and happy had never quite come.

The intermingling of pain and joy began in Mantle's first season in the major leagues. Born in Spavinaw, Oklahoma, on October 20, 1931, he needed only two years in the minor leagues before joining the Yankees in 1951—a powerful, fleet young man who could not miss being a star if a boyhood case of osteomyelitis, a bone disease, remained arrested.

That first season saw him twist his right knee on a drain

pipe while playing right field in the second game of the World Series. For the rest of the Series he was in the hospital—in the bed next to his father, who was suffering from Hodgkin's disease, which would eventually kill him.

The records show that Mantle's best years were in 1956–57, when the Yankees won pennants as usual and he was twice voted Most Valuable Player. He batted .353 in 1956, hit 52 home runs and drove in 130 runs, leading the league in all three categories, the so-called "triple crown." In 1957, he batted .365 with 34 homers and 94 runs batted in. When the Giants took Willie Mays to San Francisco after 1957, Mantle was clearly New York's biggest sports hero.

But Mantle never was at home in New York, preferring to settle in Dallas with his wife and four sons and rent homes or live in hotels during the season. And even in the best of summers, New York was not his scene. The fans saw him heave his batting helmet in disgust when he struck out and he heard as many boos as cheers.

"Me and the fans really had a go-round those first couple of years," he recalled recently. "I didn't like them and they didn't like me. But it's gotten better since then."

When fans did approach Mantle, he often did not seem to know how to react. Whereas many stars would chat with their fans—while trotting toward the sanctuary of the clubhouse—Mantle would often bolt frozen-faced through them, occasionally scattering youngsters like the halfback he wished he had been. And Mantle's reaction to the press was inconsistent and occasionally rude, although he was a funny and loyal friend to his teammates, who liked and respected him.

After the first decade, Mantle began to cope with many things, running bases, playing center field and swinging the bat with a new understanding, coupling wisdom with his physical skills.

"It seemed like I was finally getting the hang of it," he once said.

Then the injuries struck again. He tried to play the 1961 World Series with an abscess on his right buttock that oozed blood through his uniform, visible to players and fans. In 1962 he pulled a right-thigh muscle while running to first base and fell to the ground "as if he had been shot," as one reporter described it. Mantle recovered in a month from the hamstring, but he had bruised his left knee in the fall and he wound up playing only 123 games that year. Yet the Yankees won the pennant and he was voted Most Valuable Player for the third time.

The games diminished to 65 in 1963 as he broke his foot when his spikes caught in a wire fence in Baltimore. He also had knee cartilage removed in the off-season.

By 1964 it was commonly accepted by players and fans that Mantle was playing mostly on courage. Players saw him pull himself up stairways using his powerful arms to supplement his wobbly knees, and they marveled that he could play at all.

"Every time he misses, he grunts in pain," one opposing catcher said. "You think he's going to fall down."

In 1965, as the Yankees fell from first to sixth place, Mantle suffered back and neck spasms, shoulder and elbow aches and he pulled his left hamstring and missed 21 games. He had a chip removed from his right shoulder before the 1966 season, yet he insisted on opening the season in left field—to minimize his throwing. He later strained a hamstring and bruised his left hand.

By 1967, Mantle moved to first base and played in 144 games, suffering only minor aches. His average fell to .245 and his pride was hurt, but he did not quit.

"I need the money," he sometimes said, laughing as if it were a joke. But friends whispered that he needed his $100,000 salary because of poor investments, so he played on. Last year he appeared in 144 games again, this time batting only .237.

As he grew older, Mantle became extremely popular with the New York fans and he had always been adulated by fans in other cities. Last year many clubs asked if they could honor Mantle on the Yankees' final appearance in their town, just in case it was his final performance. Mantle usually said he did not want a fuss made over him and he refused the honors. He still will be honored many times,

of course, but as a retired hero rather than as a future hero
or a declining one, two roles he never thoroughly enjoyed.

20
DENNY MCLAIN:
ROLLER COASTER
PASSENGER

It's not known whether Denny McLain read
this article when it appeared in the February,
1969, issue of **Sport World.** If he did, he didn't
follow Pete Moser's suggestions.

Few baseball players have ridden a speedier
roller coaster than McLain. He followed his
31-6 year with a 24-9 mark and shared the Cy
Young American League pitching award, which
he won in 1968, with Mike Cuellar. Then it was
discovered he'd been involved in trying to
organize a betting business and was suspended
by the Commissioner of Baseball from Feb. 19
through July 1, 1970. He later threw ice water
on a sportswriter and was suspended from
Aug. 29, 1970, until the end of the season. Detroit traded him to Washington, where he led
the league in losses (22) in 1971, despite being
on the disabled list for three weeks. He was
later traded to the Oakland A's and on May 15,
1972, was optioned to Birmingham, a Class AA
team in the Southern League. The right-hander
was 3-3 at Birmingham and was recalled on
June 29 to be traded to the Atlanta Braves. He
was 3-5 with Atlanta and on Mar. 26, 1973,
McLain was placed on waivers for the purpose
of giving him his unconditional release. It was
three days before the pitcher's 29th birthday.
McLain went unclaimed and suddenly there
was plenty of time to practice on the organ,

but few requests for an individual who had been at the top of the baseball world such a short time ago.

By Pete Moser

Keep away from those kids, Denny baby. Don't push too hard on those organ keys. Watch out for the rubber chicken on the banquet circuit and watch your weight. Easy does it, Denny baby.

Denny McLain, the sensation of Detroit's first pennant-winning team in 23 years, major-league baseball's first 31-game winner in 37 years, heard it all during the fall and the winter while he was cleaning up the bucks as if he was holding vacuum cleaners in both hands. The money poured into the McLain coffers like a tidal wave.

The advice poured in, too, to the 24-year-old pitching phenom with the face and look of a dead-end kid. Denny heard it loud and clear. But Denny is a guy who rarely listens. This was cleanup time and Denny made the most of it. You couldn't blame him. It may never happen again like that.

"Pitchers just don't have many seasons like that," says Hal Newhouser, the famed former Tiger left-handed whiz. "They come once in a lifetime and maybe not even that. To win 30 games you have to have every break in the book and you can't get hurt, that's the important thing."

Newhouser had held the Tiger record of 29 wins (1944) with right-hander George Mullen (1909).

Denny got the breaks, all right, but you can't knock his fantastic season. He was the club's stopper, the winner of their big games. And, for a time, was the lone healthy and reliable starter.

You knew Denny was going to hit the magic 30 circle—the first since Dizzy Dean (30-7) of the St. Louis Cardinals in 1934 and the first in the American League since Lefty

---

Grove (31-4) in 1931—when he beat the pressing Baltimore Orioles 7-3 on Aug. 31 for victory No. 27 and moved the Tigers seven games in front of the Birds heading into the final month.

It wasn't just the victory. It was how it was done and because of one play that could have ruined McLain and the Tigers.

It came on a day when Denny, who already had pitched seven shutouts and had an ERA under 2.00, didn't have his usual stuff in the home park, a noted hitter's paradise.

McLain was having his troubles. He held a 4-3 lead in the third inning. The Orioles had scored on a walk and singles by Curt Blefary and Frank Robinson in the third for the third run.

Husky Boog Powell smashed a liner back at McLain. Denny instinctively threw up his hands and speared the vicious liner. He threw to shortstop Tom Matchick at second for the second out and Matchick's throw to Norm Cash at first finished off a triple play reeled off so fast that the fans were tongue-tied for a moment.

"It was just a reaction," recalls McLain. "If I hadn't caught it, it would have hit me in the head."

"There was no way he could catch it," says Powell. "It was a golf shot. He told me that without his contact lenses on he wouldn't have seen it. I don't think he did."

"I thought we'd knock him out," said Baltimore manager Earl Weaver then. "He didn't have any stuff but he pitched well—put the ball in some good places."

"They were hitting the hell out of my curve ball so I started throwing fastballs and sliders," says McLain. "That's been the secret of my success. I've been able to figure out what I've been doing wrong in a game and been able to make adjustments."

Manager Mayo Smith and catcher Bill Freehan both said Denny had matured and was concentrating.

It was that plus the contact lenses, a revived sidearm pitch to right-handers and the hard slider, a cross between a slider and curve which pitching coach Johnny Sain helped him to perfect.

But it was those all-important breaks. Teammate Earl

Wilson wasn't as lucky, but he too, was fortunate that his career wasn't ruined.

Wilson was hit five times by batted balls and was out of action for weeks. In one game against the Athletics in Oakland last May, he was hit in the leg and was sidelined for weeks. Then a month later in Detroit, he was struck twice in one inning with the A's. A drive off Rick Monday's bat hit Wilson on the right shoulder and then glanced off his cheek in the fifth inning. Then Reggie Jackson smashed another sizzler that hit Earl on the right hand and sent him to the hospital for X-rays.

Wilson was lucky. He came back to win some crucial games for the Tigers with his arm and bat.

You have to shudder when you think what could have happened to both McLain and Wilson. Herb Score, the brilliant, flame-throwing left-hander of the Cleveland Indians, was smashed in the face by a batted ball and his career was ended.

A bullet to the mound also curtailed Dizzy Dean's fabulous career. Three years after Dizzy won 30 as a 23-year-old, he was hit on the left toe by a line drive off the bat of Cleveland outfielder Earl Averill. The toe was fractured but 10 days later Dean came back to pitch against the Braves.

"I was favoring the toe and in one of the early innings, Bill McKechnie, the Braves' manager who was on the coaching line, yelled over to me, 'Jerome, you're going to hurt your arm pitching like that,' " recalls Dean. He was discussing McLain's bid for the 30 in September.

"Along about the seventh inning, I heard something snap in my arm. I continued to pitch but couldn't throw many fast balls after that."

A few years later, Dean's career was over. He was all washed up at 29. Now 58, and a baseball commentator, he makes more money than he did when he was a pitching great.

"When I won that 30 games, my salary was only $7,500," he remembers. "I got a raise to $18,000 the next year. Then, when I won only 28 games in 1935, Mr. Rickey (Branch Rickey, the general manager) wanted to cut my salary because I didn't win 30. I held out and got $25,500.

"You know, I was the singer with the old Mudcat Band we had back there with the Gas House Gang. There was also Pepper Martin on the guitar, Fiddler McGee, Frenchy Bordagaray on the French harp and Bob Weiland on the jug. We once went on the old Ed Wynn radio show (as popular then as the Ed Sullivan television show is now).

"I also signed for $15,000 with a food company and they used me in the funny papers. But most of the money I made in the off-season was while barnstorming with a major league All-Star team that played against Satchell Paige and his colored All-Stars. I made between $15,000 and $18,000 every year that way.

"I'm getting more publicity now about McLain trying to win 30 than when I did it," says Ole Dizzy, who really isn't dizzy at all. "There wasn't much hoopla about it back then. Nobody said a thing in the clubhouse when I won 30. We were just happy about winnin' the pennant."

Lefty Grove, now 68, says there was no fuss made about his 30th win, either. "I don't even remember who I beat. The thing I remembered best is when my 16-game winning streak was broken in St. Louis."

Television, of course, is responsible in a large measure for the changing reactions to historic feats in baseball. Television brought the games to millions of viewers who could become part of the scene. There was tremendous pressure on Roger Maris, an introvert who preferred to stay out of the limelight, when he broke Babe Ruth's home run record for a season with 61 in 1961.

Maris was dogged everywhere he went by sports writers, magazine writers, photographers and the radio and television people. Aspersion was cast on his record because he broke Ruth's record in a 162-game season, getting No. 61 in the final game.

Roger was the target of abuse from many fans who wouldn't let him forget that the famed and fun-loving Ruth had hit 60 in 154 games in 1927.

Commissioner Ford Frick also made it tougher for

Roger by declaring that an asterisk would be placed next to his record to indicate it was for a 162-game season.

This all added to pressure on Maris. He broke out in hives. His hair began to fall out. He couldn't wait for the season to end. And, eventually, he was delighted to be traded to St. Louis where he was helpful in the Cards' pennant victories of 1967 and 1968.

They didn't need any asterisks for McLain. He won No. 30 in the Tigers' 149th game. And the victory, on Sept. 14, in Detroit, was a typical one for the Tigers in the year 1968, a year in which they repeatedly won games in their last turn at bat. And that 5-4 victory was Denny's eighth against one loss in games decided by one run. He was trailing 4-3 on a six-hit, 10-strikeout effort for his 27th complete game in 38 starts when the Tigers came up for their last turn before 44,087 fans in Tiger Stadium.

Al Kaline, who finally made it into his first World Series, pinch hit for Denny and drew a walk from reliever Diego Segui. Dick McAuliffe fouled out but Mickey Stanley grounded through the box into center for a single, sending Kaline to third. Jim Northrup bounced to first baseman Danny Cater, whose throw to the plate was high and wild. This scored Kaline with the tying run and moved Stanley to third. With the infield and outfield playing close, since a fly ball would drive in the winning run, Willie Horton, the big man of the Tiger attack all season, smashed a 2-2 pitch over left fielder Jim Gosger's head for the winning run.

As Horton's hit fell in safely, McLain raced out to embrace his teammates. They, in turn, lifted Denny and marched him to the dugout. There was a wild crush around the dugout as newsmen, and photographers, television cameramen and commentators as well as fans milled around the dugout.

After McLain disappeared into the clubhouse to happily talk to interviewers, the crowd remained, yelling, "We want Denny!"

When told about it, Denny insisted on going out again to wave to the fans and acknowledge the cheers.

It seemed like years ago but it was only last May when

Denny blasted the Tiger fans "as front runners and world's worst. If people go along with us and stay off our backs, we'll win this thing." Later he amended this to say, "Only a small percentage of fans really do the booing."

Shortly after that popoff, Denny made his appearance in the home park, boasting a 5-0 record when he faced Baltimore. He was blasted out of the box for the first time of the season as the Orioles lumped the Tigers 10-8. Denny lasted two innings in that May 15 contest.

The booing started during his warm-ups.

"I've been booed before, but never like that," he said then, "and I guess it made me press too hard."

It wasn't long after that when McLain disclosed that his wife Sharyn, daughter of former big league star and manager Lou Boudreau, and their 2-year-old daughter, Kristi, narrowly escaped possible serious injury after someone in Detroit placed a smoke bomb in the family car.

McLain said his wife was driving from Tiger Stadium to their suburban home when she pulled off the highway to get gas.

"The attendant looked under the hood and discovered there was a smoke bomb wired to the ignition," he said. "If the bomb had gone off when my wife was driving at high speed, she and the baby could have been killed. But the bomb wasn't wired properly, fortunately. It was supposed to go off when the ignition was turned on.

"If anything had happened I'd have spent the rest of my life finding out who was responsible."

At that time the fans still were smarting from the Tigers' folderoo in 1967 and Denny's vital part in the flop. He had won 17 games and appeared headed for another 20-game winning season (20-16 in 1966). That would have meant the flag for the Tigers, winless since 1945. But he suffered two dislocated toes in his own living room, caused, he said, when he stood up after his foot had fallen asleep while he was watching television. Apparently the fans didn't buy this. Anyway, he didn't pitch until the final day when the Tigers lost the pennant by one game.

You've got to hand it to Denny. He shouldered a good

part of the blame for the loss. In spring training, he said things were going to be different in '68. They were. Denny got off rolling and so did the club. Except for a couple of challenges by the Orioles, it was smooth sailing for the Tigers. The jeers changed to cheers for Denny and the other Tigers from June on.

Denny took it all in stride. He was as brash, talkative and controversial as ever. He wasn't labeled "Mighty Mouth" for nothing. This time the fans could take it because he was putting up if he wasn't shutting up.

What made the big difference? The low ERA? The almost 5-1 ratio between strikeouts and walks? The ability to get the big out?

Denny believes it began in spring training when he used contact lenses instead of spectacles for the first time. ("I can't see across the table without glasses," he says.) In 1967, he seemed to be always adjusting his glasses. Sweat made them slip on his nose.

"With the contacts I can focus easier and it helped me improve my concentration. I know it made me a better all-around pitcher."

What also helped was his development of the hard slider and his renewed use of the sidearm pitch to right-handed hitters.

The 5-11, 185-pound right-hander had thrown the sidearm pitch until he injured a shoulder muscle later in the 1965 season. He began throwing it early in the '68 season and it had the right-handers baffled.

Pitching coach Johnny Sain helped him with the hard slider. McLain's slider used to be a gopher ball. He was whacked for 42 homers in 1966 and 35 in 1967, most of them on hanging sliders.

"It got so bad that I forgot about the slider completely," he says. With Sain's help, he changed his delivery on the slider. "It became my miracle ball," he says. "It would get me double plays and strikeouts."

"Denny has always known what he can do with a base-ball," says Sain, who had much success with the Yankee and Twins' pitching staffs before coming to Detroit under Mayo Smith. "He just learned the technique of doing it correctly. He knows when to throw a rising fastball instead of a sinking fastball, when to throw a change-up instead of a curve. He learned to concentrate."

"He's helped me," says McLain of Sain. "But I can't really describe to you how. The outlook is the main thing. It has to do with positive thinking. He has a way of building your confidence, and showing you how to think right, and concentrate. He helps with mechanical things, too, but the main thing is mental. I guess part of it is just the respect you come to feel for him."

"Denny's record speaks for itself," says manager Mayo Smith, who almost traded him to Baltimore for shortstop Luis Aparicio in the winter preceding the pennant year. "His concentration, his slider and his control have done it. And, besides all that, he's a hell of a competitor. He has risen to the occasion every time."

The "occasion" included three wins by McLain when he was called on to start after only two days of rest because of the depletion of the pitching staff in June and July.

"He's in a fantastic groove," said Boston's Jim Lonborg when Denny was rolling along at a fast clip. "Once you get in a groove like that, everything seems to go right."

Lonborg should know. He was the AL's Pitcher of the Year in 1967 when he posted a 22-9 record in leading the amazing Red Sox to the pennant. But after the World Series Lady Luck turned the other way on Lonborg. He spilled while skiing on Dec. 23 and tore two ligaments in his right knee. The surgery and the rehabilitation program ruined his season and knocked the Red Sox right out of the 1968 race.

Lonborg's words of advice, if any are needed for Denny on that score, are to stay off the skis.

Another Boston hero, Triple Crown batting king Carl Yastrzemski, warned Denny not to try and grab everything in sight during the off-season. Carl cleaned up with his many awards, endorsements and financially rewarding banquet talks at $1,000 per and up.

"Denny better be careful," Carl said. "It can swallow you up."

He told Joe Falls, the crack Detroit columnist, that "I scheduled six banquets—just six. Do you know how many I went to? I made 24 banquets in January alone. I went to Seattle and made 15 appearances in one day. I did an airline commercial and they flew me to half a dozen cities in four days.

"I woke up one day and we were in Winter Haven for the start of spring training and I couldn't believe it. I couldn't believe the winter was over. I was mentally beat."

Yaz got off slowly and it wasn't until mid-season that he really got going. The Sox never got into the race and Yaz never came close to his figures of 1967.

Denny, a first class organist, who has been playing since he was eight, had enough loot-making engagements lined up for him by agent Frank Scott to make even Bob Hope look for the end of the road.

Denny's father, a pianist and organist, taught Denny how to play the organ. His father died when he was 13 and Denny says he started making money playing the organ that year. He's a real pro at it.

Late in the '68 season, he gave a recital in New York at the swank Hampshire House on Central Park South. He's under contract to the Hammond Organ company. He was booked everywhere. The money rolled in.

"Where a Mantle or a Maris could command only $1,000 or $1,500 an appearance because they were limited to saying a few words," says agent Frank Scott, "McLain can play the organ and get $2,500."

Before he started cashing in, McLain was smart enough to say that "I know I can only make this kind of money outside of the playing field because of what I do inside those white lines."

Now if he only remembers his own words of caution, Denny really might be on the road to greatness or another super year, at least.

21
STEVE CARLTON:
BUSCH'S FOLLY

When the New York Mets won the National League championship in 1973 they finished 1½ games ahead of St. Louis in the race for top honors in their division. In 1974 the Cardinals were again edged out as Pittsburgh finished 1½ games ahead of the Redbirds in the NL's East Division. But how would the team have made out if St. Louis owner Gussie Busch had not become angry over contract negotiations with Steve Carlton and sent him to Philadelphia in exchange for pitcher Rick Wise?

Carlton didn't achieve his 1973 goal of 30 wins mentioned in Bus Saidt's article, but there's no doubt the Phillies were winners in their deal for the pitcher. Carlton was 13-20 in 1973, while Wise was 16-12 although their earned run averages were similar. In 1974 Carlton led the National League in strikeouts with 240 and was second in complete games with 17. Only six pitchers in the league topped his win total of 16. Wise wasn't one of them. He had been traded to the Red Sox and appeared in only nine games because of arm problems.

By Bus Saidt

"Getting base hits off Steve Carlton," said Willie Stargell, the big blaster of the Pittsburgh Pirates, minutes after Carlton had blanked the Bucs, 2-0, for his 13th straight victory in what was to become a 15-game winning streak, "is like trying to drink coffee with a fork."

Sometimes a few words are worth a thousand pictures.

As the unofficial spokesman of the National League hitters' union, Stargell succeeded in placing the 1972 baseball season of Super Steve, the magnificent Philadelphia Phillies' southpaw, in exact perspective.

In the City of Brotherly Love, where losing professional athletic teams and sub-standard individual performances are a way of life, like crime in the streets, increased cost of living and growing traffic problems, Steve Carlton stood out like Billy Penn's statue which sets off Philadelphia's skyline atop City Hall.

Carlton is the Phillies' franchise. Without him, the club might not have finished the season. It might have disappeared into thin air, unmissed and unmourned.

With him enjoying one of the greatest seasons any pitcher has experienced in the history of the game, the worst club in the league attracted 1,343,329 customers through the turnstiles at Veterans Stadium.

"It's really impossible to say exactly how individual-game attendance was affected the times when Steve was scheduled to start," said Bill Giles, Phillies' executive vice-president, "but it wouldn't be out of line to say that perhaps as much as half our home attendance might be attributed directly to his appearances."

Carlton's incredible performance is not going unrewarded. Almost as quickly as the bartender could pour the Jack Daniel's in Director of Player Personnel Paul Owens' glass and open Carlton's bottle of beer, Steve had agreed to work another year for a reported $165,000.

"I told Paul I feel I should be the highest paid pitcher in baseball," said Carlton matter-of-factly, "and he agreed. And that was that."

Since there was no outcry of protest from Carlton's former employer, the St. Louis Cardinals, and Bullet Bob Gibson, heretofore recognized as the pitcher earning the highest yearly salary, it seems safe to assume that Steve's wish was Owens' command.

Carlton thus moves into the nice neighborhood of the

$100,000-plus pitchers which includes Gibson, Juan Marichal, Ferguson Jenkins, Tom Seaver and Wilbur Wood.

"The bulk of my salary is immediately invested," explained Carlton, whose financial affairs are handled by a California management firm headed by LaRue Harcourt. "The main concern is how much money do I get to keep?

"Both my wife and I work off monthly allowances."

Signing contracts under such euphoric circumstances hasn't always been common to the Carlton cause. In fact, it was Cardinal owner Gussie Busch's total disenchantment with the salary haggling on the part of many of his hired hands which ultimately led to the decision to trade Carlton for Rick Wise.

The handsome left-hander, a cinch to play himself when Hollywood films "The Steve Carlton Story," had settled on a two-year contract after winning 14 games in 1967. He won 13 in '68 and 17 in '69 and then the trouble started.

There was a long holdout in early 1970, followed by a hard-to-believe 10-19 record. "I got to spring training late and everything went wrong all year," Steve said.

By the close of the '70 season, beer baron Busch began to think he had been too generous with his baseball employees. When Carlton said thanks, but no thanks, to the contract General Manager Bing Devine mailed him in January of 1971, Busch hit the ceiling.

"I remember the first time I heard we had a chance to get Steve," said Owens, a glazed look crossing his eyes like a man who still didn't believe such largesse was possible. "As long as I live I'll never forget that day.

"It was my wedding anniversary and we were having dinner with John and Ma Quinn (the former Phillies' general manager and his wife) at Heilman's Beachcomber in Clearwater Beach.

"John asked me, 'What would you say to a Wise-for-Carlton deal?' My first reaction was to say, 'John, you've had one too many.' I thought he was kidding.

"I mean Rick Wise was a 17-game winner for us and one of the most popular ballplayers in Philadelphia, but

Steve Carlton? Hell, I always thought of him as having a chance to be the best pitcher in baseball—and he was a left-hander in the bargain."

Quinn wasn't kidding and neither was Devine. Two days later, Carlton became a Phillie in what must be termed one of the most fortuitous turns of events in Phillies' history.

"It was strictly a matter of money," insisted Jim Toomey, Devine's assistant. "We were about $15,000 apart in February last year. The final decision was made by Mr. Busch and Dick Meyer, our executive vice-president.

"Steve's a good guy and there never was any problem wtih him except when it came to dough. I guess Mr. Busch just got tired of arguing with him all the time."

Carlton, although not all that thrilled about being shuffled off to a city of losers, accepted his fate like a pro. He was genuinely surprised, however, that Busch was the driving force behind banishing him from St. Louis.

"Bing Devine's the general manager," Steve said the day he showed up in Clearwater in Phillies' candy-stripes. "He makes the deals."

Curiously, Philadelphia baseball writers, generally accepted by their peers as being among the more astute and talented in the baseball writing fraternity, were not overly thrilled by the Wise-Carlton trade.

"The Phillies' switchboard has been jammed all day," typed one of them. "People are canceling ticket reservations like mad. Rick Wise is their boy."

At best, the trade was considered a standoff.

"I'd say Wise will match Carlton's 20 wins with the Cards before Steve equals Rick's 17 with the Phils," wrote one of the nation's foremost scribes, Dick Young, of the *New York Daily News*.

Baseball men tended to think more of Wise than Carlton. Players leaned toward Carlton.

"I expect Rick Wise to be a more consistent pitcher than Carlton from here on out," predicted the late Gil Hodges.

"I like Wise's steady improvement," said the New York Mets' General Manager, Bob Scheffing.

But Met shortstop Buddy Harrelson, echoing the sentiments of many players queried in the St. Petersburg-Tampa-Clearwater spring training triangle, said, "You mean to say the Phillies got Carlton for Wise straight up? That's hard to believe. Nobody in the league throws better or harder than Steve. He's one of the best, without putting Wise down."

Carlton provided the answer to the debate by establishing himself as the best pitcher in baseball. The 28-year-old southpaw was 27-10 with a league-leading ERA of 1.98. On the way, he set two league records—most victories for a hurler of a last-place team and highest percentage of a team's games won, 46 per cent tied Sandy Koufax's mark of most wins by a left-hander, 27, set nine Philadelphia club records and led the National League in starts (41), complete games (30), wins (27), innings pitched (346), strikeouts (310), ERA (1.98), facing most batsmen (1,351), fewest opponents hits (257). His eight shutouts were second to the Dodgers' Don Sutton, who had nine.

When he showed up at the gala Chicago dinner to receive the S. Rae Hickok Belt as Professional Athlete-of-the-Year, Carlton had shaved off his very long, droopy, Fu Manchu mustache.

"I was shocked when I saw him without it," said his pretty wife, Beverly, whom he met while pitching at Winnipeg in 1964 and who is the mother of their two children, Steve, Jr., 7, and Scott, 3. "He never said a word to me about it.

"He must have taken it off between the time he started to get dressed to come downstairs for the dinner and the time the affair began."

The planners who run the country's winter sports banquets quite properly rushed to the Steve Carlton bandwagon. He was the pro athlete of the year according to the Philadelphia Sportswriters Association. He was presented the Clark Griffin Memorial Award by the Washington, D.C. Touchdown Club. And he won the Sid

Mercer Player-of-the-Year award at the New York Baseball Writers Dinner.

The Phillies' brass set down an eight-banquet schedule for the club's meal ticket so as not to run him into the ground fulfilling social demands.

"I don't enjoy public speaking," Steve said, "but I do appreciate all the honors. I guess I'll never be a comedian. I got up at the New York writers' dinner and said that Bing Devine had just been named Man-of-the-Year by beating out Mark Spitz.

"It was supposed to be funny, but nobody laughed."

Carlton is a basically even-tempered young man, although he has been known to go slightly berserk with old buddies like Tim McCarver, Joe Hoerner and Dal Maxvill after particularly galling defeats.

He is an occasional golfer who loves to hunt and fish. Otherwise, he is pretty much a homebody. Despite his newfound credentials to join the nouveau riche class, Carlton and his family still occupy the modest, shingle house near St. Louis for which they paid $25,000 in 1968.

"Steve is a pretty terrific guy," according to his wife, not exactly an unbiased source. "He's a very earthy type when he's at home.

"I always said to him, 'Steve, if you ever get to be really successful as a baseball player, please don't forget all the other people you've known while you were getting there.'

"And I can honestly say he's just as great as he always was. Strictly down-to-earth."

Carlton's super success story is based technically on complete command of three basic pitches, the fastball, slider and curve.

There are no gimmicks in his pitching arsenal. He is the boss out there, and he knows it. So do the hitters, as Willie Stargell stated so aptly.

"No pitcher since Koufax has mastered three pitches as well as Steve," said his pitching coach, Ray Rippelmeyer. "And I'm not sure Sandy's slider was up to Steve's."

Carlton first began "fooling around" with the slider while touring Japan with the Cardinals after the 1968 World Series. He used it effectively in '69, but junked it the next two seasons.

"I just couldn't seem to throw it right," he said. "And then it started hurting my arm when I threw it."

But Rippelmeyer urged him to try it again last spring, and the results were devastating to the hitters.

It's startling, but true, that Carlton's 27-10 season easily could have been 30-8 or better. He was off to a 5-1 beginning, then dropped five straight decisions.

"In every one of those defeats," Carlton said, "I started dropping my wrist on my breaking ball. It was strictly a matter of not sustaining my concentration.

"Pitching successfully is essentially mind over matter, thinking positively, and controlling those three pitches."

Carlton never once complained about pitching for a lowly, disorganized club like the Phillies, who fired their general manager and field manager during the 1972 season and played their way to the National League's cellar.

While the team seemed to play better baseball when Carlton was pitching, their lack of offense is painfully apparent. In his ten losses, the Phillies scored just 16 runs, or 1.6 per game.

Carlton and his wife credit a strange, remote, elderly man they call "Briggs" with turning the great pitcher's career around from threatened mediocrity to unparalleled success.

"It was '70, the year I lost 19 games," he remembered. "Everything was going wrong.

"I received this ten-page letter from this man down in Texas. He told me he was tired of seeing a pitcher he said was as talented as me keep losing so much.

"Normally I might have read the first couple of sentences and thrown it away. But there was something almost mysterious about this letter that got to me.

"It had a lot of information dealing with the mind and positive thinking. These were the thoughts of a very profound man. His inner knowledge was remarkable. He quoted from philosophers and the Bible and made life truly positive and beautiful.

"He began writing me once a week and I still hear from him regularly.

"Whenever I have some kind of personal problem, I always turn to my old friend for advice. Just call him 'Briggs.' Our relationship is too personal to give his full name and where he is now."

"Briggs's" influence probably is responsible for the ultra-confident manner in which Carlton faces the new baseball season.

"My goal is to win 30 games this year," he said. "I might even accomplish that in 29 starts.

"The mental approach will be the same this year, but the knowledge has expanded. I don't plan to change a thing. Those extra demands created by winning won't take a thing away from me.

"There's no way I could get off to a bad start. I simply won't permit it.

"Defeat? I never consider it. Pressure? It doesn't exist in my mind. Pressure is a variable I refuse to recognize. If there is such a thing as pressure, it's on the hitters to hit me, not for me to get them out."

The first unanimous Cy Young Award winner since Gibson in 1968 does not mind admitting he will take a drink or two.

"During the season," he said, "I like to unwind by going out and having a few drinks after a game, win or lose. Otherwise, I might lie in bed all night long without sleeping.

"Most of my drinking is done during the baseball season. I might go two or three weeks in the off-season without touching a drop.

"Hard liquor has been a part of my life since I was a kid growing up on the fringes of the Everglades in North Miami. I guess I started on vodka and beer when I was around 14. We used to kick over a few moonshine stills to get our jollies."

Steve is the only son of Joe and Anne Carlton who also have two daughters. The family lived in the semi-tropical scrub of Miami where Joe Carlton worked as a member of Pan American Airways maintenance crews.

He virtually was forced into playing baseball.

"I was 15 and 6-3 and about 185 pounds when I was in ninth grade in high school," Steve recalled. "I didn't play with a lot of kids. I was very shy, and I didn't like meeting other kids.

"I had a newspaper route, and I was making a little glue (money). Right then I wasn't too interested in becoming a pitcher. They practically had to drag me down to the field.

"But I always could throw like hell—anything I could get a grip on. Rabbits were my favorite target, but I used to knock doves right off telephone wires. I've even knocked a bird right off the top of a tree with a baseball.

"Now you're going to say this is a tall story, but it's true. One day I was walking through the brush with an axe and I saw a quail up in a tree. I threw the axe, and it cut off that quail's head and stuck right in the tree.

"It wasn't mean or cruel in those days. I might have been 12 or 13. We kids didn't think there was any difference bringing down a gamebird with a rock or a ball than with a gun.

"It was nothing to go out and come home with rattlesnakes, copperheads or corals. One day I caught a seven-foot alligator."

Cardinal area scout John Buyk took Steve to Chase Riddle who introduced the 19-year-old kid to Howie Pollet. They paid him $5,000 to sign. The long road to fame began in 1964 at Rock Hill in the Carolina League.

He reached the top of the mountain last year on August 17 when he beat Cincinnati, 9-4, for his 15th straight victory and 20th of the season. More than 53,000 Philadelphia fans, longing for some athlete to idolize, called him back for encore after encore.

"There never will be anything to top that night," Carlton said. "That was a whole lifetime in one night."

It was the late Charlie Dressen, upon seeing the young Willie Mays make an impossible throw to home plate to cut down Billy Cox, who growled, "Not a bad play, but I'd like to see him do it again."

Were Charlie around today, he'd likely be expressing the same cynicism over Steve Carlton's 27 victories of last year.

Well, anyway, Willie Stargell and the rest of the National League hitters still will be going out for their coffee, with Steve Carlton pouring.

The question is: Will they be using spoons or forks with which to drink it?

22
EDDIE STANKY:
BIG LITTLE MAN

Eddie Stanky accomplished what may have been the only successful drop kick in the history of baseball. He was going to be an easy out at second base, but shocked Phil Rizzuto by knocking the ball loose with a good stiff kick to the glove hand. The play was a vital one. It helped the New York Giants score five runs in the fifth inning en route to a 6-1 triumph over the Yankees in the third game of the 1951 World Series. Stanky could only play the game one way—flat out. He later found this to be a problem. As he tried to manage, he was nonplussed to discover that other players didn't perform with his enthusiasm.

By Whitney Martin

He stood there, a compact little guy impeccably attired. The strong hands that held the plaque were without tremor, and his eyes were steady and fearless. He spoke slowly and clearly, choosing his words carefully:

"As I look at these great players in front of me I never felt so insignificant in my life . . ."

And you thought of Eddie Stanky on the baseball field, a scratching, clawing wildcat ripping into Len Merullo, a former buddy who now was playing on another team, and consequently was an enemy.

"I doubt if there ever was a player with less ability who received this award . . ."

And you recalled Eddie Stanky, an agitated bundle of concentrated fury, throwing his cap to the ground and leaping up and down in uncontrolled rage at what he considered an unfair decision by an umpire in a World Series.

"But you may be sure that, although nobody with less ability ever has received or ever will receive this award, I can vouch that no one ever has been or ever will be more appreciative . . ."

There flashed before you the picture of Eddie Stanky, with cold and calculated insolence, pushing his way between the catcher and umpire on his way to the plate, his studied nonchalance infuriating in its semblance of innocence.

"I want to thank you for appreciating my intangibles on the field . . ."

You saw him again, stretching and waving his arms in impromptu calisthenics, his energetic gyrations just accidentally being in the line of vision of a Phillie batter who was having trouble enough following the ball as it was.

"This is the first time I have been introduced without them saying I can't hit, can't run, and can't throw . . ."

And you thought of the many, many times the little guy came up with stops out there at second base bordering on the impossible, and of the many, many times he came through with that game-winning single, or double, after driving a pitcher wild with plate antics calculated to do just that.

The little New York Giant keystoner with moods varying from articulate, unbridled fury to cold, calculated and silent needling of his bitter enemies, who were any players who happened to be on the opposing team, was rated by the New York Baseball Writers the outstanding player of 1950, and you can't argue very stoutly against the choice.

He himself hit the bull's-eye when he referred to his "intangibles." In so many subtle ways, aside from the recognized hitting, fielding or throwing, he influenced the play.

It was Eddie Stanky's spirit which held the club together during the early days of the season when nothing seemed to go right. It was his remorseless quest for victory, achieved at any cost. He had no friends other than his teammates once he put on his uniform.

But when he took it off and donned civvies, the transformation was astounding. Quiet, easy-spoken, intelligent, he would grace any gathering, as he did the Writers' Banquet at which he received belated homage.

You had to stretch your imagination to see in this little gentleman holding the plaque the implacable competitor who asked no quarter on the ball field, the man who would coldly and maliciously ram a baseball down a base runner's throat if it would help win a game.

The little guy plays the game for keeps, and when it is over he forgets about animosities of the heat of battle. You'd want him on your side. What more can you say?

23
TOMMIE AGEE: MOMENT TO REMEMBER

Two days after this 1969 article left Phil Pepe's typewriter, New York City had one of the wildest celebrations in its history. The New York Mets surprised the Baltimore Orioles and won baseball's world championship in five games. The Series was filled with spectacular defensive plays by the Mets, who had never finished higher than ninth place since entering the National League in 1962. Tommie Agee, the hero of Pepe's story, had joined the Mets in 1968 after being named the American League's Rookie of the Year with Cleveland in 1966. Following the 1972 season he was traded to the Houston Astros and later claimed the Mets "became fat cats" after their victory. When the Mets won another league title in 1973, Agee was soon to be out of baseball and running a tavern near Shea Stadium—where he had performed the heroics Phil Pepe describes here.

By Phil Pepe

A city that has seen Joe DiMaggio and Willie Mays play center field—and figured it had seen it all—now has seen Tommie Agee. Not once, but twice. Agee went to his right, then went to his left, and came up with a pair of spectacular catches that will rank among the greatest in World Series history.

The two catches saved the Mets five runs, exactly their margin of victory as they blanked the Orioles, 5–0, in Shea yesterday and took a 2–1 lead in the best-of-seven Series to crown baseball's 1969 World Champion. With their aces, Tom Seaver and Jerry Koosman, ready to pitch games four and five, the Mets figure they can wrap it up in five and avoid a return trip to Baltimore.

Rookie right-hander Gary Gentry, just a week past his 23rd birthday, got credit for the victory with saves going to Nolan Ryan and Agee. Gentry departed with the bags loaded and two out in the seventh, and Ryan came in to wrap up the four-hit shutout.

The Mets have caught the Orioles in a batting slump or, depending on your point of view, the Met pitchers have silenced Oriole sticks. The Birds have scored five runs and made only 12 hits in three games. Over the last 22 innings, Met pitchers have held them to one run and six hits.

It was obvious this would be Agee's day right from the start. After Gentry retired the Orioles in the first, Tommie led off for the Mets and drilled Jim Palmer's 2-1 fast ball over the center wall. It was his first hit in the Series and emphasized the reason manager Gil Hodges likes to have Agee leading off. It's an old Casey Stengel idea, hoping to grab a psychological advantage with a big hit to start the game.

Four times during the season Agee led the game with a homer. The Mets won three of those games. Having given the Mets the lead in this important third game, Agee was determined to keep the Orioles from taking it away. He was to get his chance in the fourth.

By then the Mets had jumped out to a 3–0 lead, the second and third runs coming from a most unexpected source. Gentry had driven them in with a double over the head of a rather surprised Paul Blair in center.

Gary's big blast came after Jerry Grote walked and Bud Harrelson singled with two out. Then Gentry jumped on Palmer's first pitch, a high fast ball, that landed at the start of the warning track some 10 feet in front of the 396-foot sign slightly to the right of center. The hit was Gentry's first since August 3. He had failed to hit in his last 28 at bats and had driven in one run all year.

Buzzing the ball for three innings, Gentry had retired the Birds without a hit. Then, after he got Blair looking to start the fourth, Frank Robinson lashed a rocket to left. At first, Cleon Jones seemed to back off to play it safe. Then, as if realizing the Orioles were hitless, he dashed in and tried a shoestring catch. Left-field ump Hank Soar ruled Cleon had trapped the ball and Robby was on with the Birds' first hit.

When Boog Powell followed with a hit through the right side, the Orioles were in business. But Gentry threw hard stuff and buzzed a third strike past Brooks Robinson and faced lefty-swinging catcher Elrod Hendricks.

Playing Hendricks to pull, Agee was over in right center and deep but Ellie crossed him up by hitting the ball hard the other way. With a crack of the bat, everybody was running—Agee to left center and the two Oriole base runners tearing around the infield.

After going full speed for about 40 yards, Tommie caught up with the ball near the fence, reached out backhanded and caught the ball in the webbing of his glove about waist high. It was a catch that veteran press-box observers were rating over Mays' back-to-the-plate grab of Vic Wertz's drive in the 1954 Series, Al Gionfriddo's steal against Joe DiMaggio in the 1947 Series and Sandy Amoros' one-hand grab of Yogi Berra's opposite field shot in the 1955 Series.

It was a catch that electrified the crowd of 56,335, including the distinguished gray-haired gentleman sitting in Commissioner Bowie Kuhn's box to the left of the Mets' dugout. The man's name is Joe DiMaggio.

It was a catch that Agee almost didn't make. "The ball," he said, "almost went through my webbing."

It was a catch that saved at least two runs and protected the Mets' 3–0 lead.

It was a catch that brought the inevitable press-box crack, "I'd like to see him do it again," a parody of a line Charlie Dressen once delivered after Willie Mays made one of his unbelievable grabs against the Dodgers. In this case, the quipster had to wait just three more innings to see Agee do it again.

The Mets upped their lead to 4–0 in the sixth when Grote cracked a double to left to deliver Ken Boswell, who had singled and moved to second as Ed Kranepool grounded out to the right side.

Gentry was still firing zips when the Birds came to bat in the seventh. Hendricks drove deep to center and Davey Johnson did likewise. Then, with two out and nobody on, Gentry was bitten by wildness. He failed to find the plate against Mark Belanger. He also walked pinch-looker Dave May, then loaded the bases by throwing four off the plate to Don Buford.

With Blair, the tying run, coming to bat and Gentry

obviously tiring, Hodges reached into his pen for smoke-thrower Nolan Ryan, the 22-year-old right-hander who was the hero of the third play-off game against the Braves.

Everybody in the park knew what Ryan was going to do—throw bullets. Blair looked at the first lightning bolt, then swung and missed at the second lightning bolt. Now the Mets were one strike away from getting out of the inning.

But Blair hit the next fast ball and it went out faster than it had come in, heading for the alley in right center. Three runners took off and so did Tommie Agee.

This time he didn't have to run very far. This time he did not have to reach across his body. This time he had only to dive headlong with his glove outstretched and scoop the ball just before it hit the running track. Tommie Agee had done it again, had saved three runs, had taken the heart out of the Orioles' attack.

Kranepool's smash over the center-field wall off Dave Leonhard in the eighth made it 5–0 for the Mets as Ryan went out to pitch the ninth.

Hendricks and Johnson, the first two Bird hitters in the ninth, kept the ball away from Agee and flied to right, but Ryan walked Belanger after having him 0-2. Clay Dalrymple batted for Leonhard and stroked one up the middle that Al Weis smothered, but he couldn't get the ball to Harrelson in time to force Belanger. When Buford followed with a walk, Hodges also walked—to the mound.

The bases were loaded. The tying run was in the on-deck circle and his name was Frank Robinson. In the Mets' pen, ace relievers Tug McGraw and Ron Taylor were warmed and ready to go, and Hodges had to know the Orioles possessed the firepower to wipe out a 5–0 lead in a hurry. They had done it many times during the season. Once, against the Tigers, they had belted three straight homers, a double and a single to turn a 5–2 defeat into a 6–5 victory.

When Hodges returned to the Mets' dugout, he came back without Ryan. It was up to the kid from Alvin, Texas, to pitch the Mets out of one more jam.

Again Ryan threw two lightning bolts to get ahead of Blair, 0-2. The situation was the same as it had been in the seventh, but this time Ryan didn't need Tommie Agee. Instead of smoke, Ryan crackled a curve ball over the plate and the game ended with Blair's bat on his shoulder. The man had made the right move once again.

Long after Blair watched the third strike snake over the plate, they were still talking of Agee's catches, comparing them with Amoros' and Mays' and Gionfriddo's and comparing them with each other. The consensus was: both great.

Tommie Agee, who had done it all for the Mets all season, but had done little in the first two games of the Series, was the man for the Mets yesterday. They asked him if he liked the home run or the catches better.

"The home run meant only one run," Tommie said. "The catches meant more. I think I'd rather have caught the two balls than hit the home run."

Naturally, he'll take the catches and the homer. At the plate he was Batman. In the field he was Robin. Because of Tommie Agee, the Orioles today are sick birds.

24
JIM BUNNING:
HAPPY FATHER'S DAY

Much is said about a difference between the American and National League strike zones. Whatever the difference may be, it didn't make much difference to Jim Bunning. He found strikes just as easy to pitch in both leagues. He struck out 201 batters in a season twice with the Detroit Tigers and fanned 219 at the age of 33 with the Philadelphia Phillies. It was during the latter season that he produced one of baseball's rarer accomplishments—a perfect game.

Bunning's name doesn't come up as much as

it should when people talk about pitching stars of the past 25 years. When he retired, he had started more games than Whitey Ford or Bob Feller (519); had as many shutouts as Sandy Koufax (40); won more games than Don Drysdale (224); and at the start of the 1975 season was third on the all-time strikeout list (2,855) behind Walter Johnson and Bob Gibson.

By Ray Robinson

It has become popular to assume that anything can and will happen at Shea Stadium, the home of the New York Mets. The assumption is based part on persistent press agentry and part on performance.

On Father's Day, June 21, 1964, a very hot Sunday in New York, when anyone with a bathing suit and the price of a trip to the beach was lolling at the seashore—that is, anyone who wasn't a Mets fan—something unusual *did* occur in Casey Stengel's solarium. A tall, right-handed pitcher named Jim Bunning, with a keen eye for the shifting fortunes of the stock market and an even keener eye for the dimensions of home plate, threw a total of 90 pitches in nine innings. Only 21 of them were balls. The rest were strikes, fouls or were hit for outs.

The result: the first perfect game in the National League since someone named John Ward licked Buffalo back in June, 1880. Someone else named Don Larsen, more likely to be remembered by the current crop of ball fans, spun his perfectionist magic in 1956, for the Yanks against the Brooklyn Dodgers in the World Series. Until Jim Bunning consumed less than two-and-a-half hours anesthetizing the Mets, in behalf of the Philadelphia Phillies, nobody in either league had bothered equalling Larsen's perfect game. And before Larsen had done it, you had to go all the way back to Charley Robertson's 1922 game against the Detroit Tigers, to find a no-hit, no-run, no-man-on ball game.

In other words, Jim Bunning really made Shea Stadium live up to its press notices. Yet, despite the fact that Bunning pitched the most talked-about, most publicized single game of the 1964 season, he would probably have turned the whole thing in for a routine 20th victory.

The reason is quite simple and has nothing to do with Bunning's aversion to perfection or the ultimate in pitching prowess. His team lost the National League flag to the Cards by a single game. In the last two weeks of the season, when the Phillies melted away like snowballs in the late summer sun, Jim, working sometimes with only two days rest, couldn't produce a victory. Then, on the final day of the campaign he shut out the Cincinnati Reds for his 19th win. Perfect games, shutouts, schmutouts—he would have settled for a mediocre 12-11 triumph, if it could have meant the pennant for his club.

"Am I satisfied?" said Bunning on the afternoon the season came to its harrowing end. "I should say not. We didn't win the pennant. And that's what we had in mind ten days ago."

In June, when he baffled the Mets with his assortment of sidearm strikes and sliders, both Bunning and the Phils were riding high. Gene Mauch had his team in first place, Bunning already had won seven games ("When he loses, we are shocked," said Dennis Bennett, then a fellow worker of Jim's) and the Mets were performing with the perfect futility everyone expected of them.

As the fans crowded into Shea Stadium that day— 32,026 of them were on hand, including Jim's wife, Mary, and his oldest daughter, 12-year-old Barbara—Manager Mauch had a sneaking suspicion this was going to be more than an ordinary game.

He watched from the dugout as Bunning went through his warmup ritual. Maybe it was hindsight, but Mauch recalled later for the press that Jim seemed "special."

"The way he was throwing, so live and as high as he was. Not high with his pitches. High—himself," said Mauch.

When the game started, Bunning faced the Mets lead-offer Jim Hickman. He threw him two balls that Jim fouled off, both sliders. Then, audaciously, he laughed in Hickman's face, and shouted down at him from his lofty perch on the mound: "You won't get any more like that!"

On the next pitch, Hickman struck out. It was a perfect start to a perfect afternoon.

Once Jesse Gonder, the Mets catcher, hit a hard shot into the hole between first and second base. But agile Tony Taylor was there to gobble it up and throw him out with a good throw. That was the closest the Mets came to a hit all day.

As the game progressed everyone realized Bunning was working to be the perfect Daddy on Daddy's Day. What more could he present to his Missus and his four girls and three boys?

From the fifth inning on, Jim was so aware of his budding masterpiece, that he almost led cheers from the dugout. He exhorted his mates, jabbered incessantly, paced back and forth, tabulated aloud how many outs he had to go for the perfecto, tried to relax by talking about the event. In other words, he did everything to defy protocol and the time-honored superstition that ballplayers don't like to talk about no-hitters while they're happening.

"I knew I had a chance after Tony made that play on Gonder," said Bunning. "If you talk about it you're not as disappointed, if you don't get it."

The way the Mets were walking up there and then sitting down, there didn't seem to be much doubt that Bunning would get what he was chirping about. But even one error in this type of game could spoil Bunning's effort and that meant that the pressure was on everyone in a Philly uniform, not alone Bunning.

"When I heard Jim," said John Briggs, the first-year center fielder, "I kept telling myself that if I had to I'd dive ten feet for the ball." Bunning, however, made such strenuous effort unnecessary.

In the late innings Jim motioned to his infielders and outfielders where to play, much as Mauch himself might.

But Mauch didn't resent such usurpation from his crew-cutted hurler. "I think he did it as much to relax himself as he did it to relax his teammates," said the understanding manager.

By the ninth inning, Bunning was so high and hopeful, his catcher, Gus Triandos, could only describe him as "silly."

"I'd like to have Koufax's fast one right now," he laughed, as he trudged to the mound to begin his last mile. He had to get Charlie Smith, George Altman and whoever Stengel would nominate to bat for pitcher Tom Sturdivant.

Smith obliged by popping one up in foul territory to shortstop Bobby Wine. One out. The normally partisan Met crowd roared its approval of the enemy pitcher. Altman swung at a low curve for Bunning's ninth strikeout and you would have thought the Mets had just won the flag.

Now Johnny Stephenson, a lefty, came up to challenge Bunning's big ball game. This young man hasn't broken up many games in his time and maybe in their hearts, to borrow that unfortunate political slogan, the Mets were hoping the kid would get it over with quickly. But in baseball you play it all out, even when you're behind 6-0 and a guy has a fortune riding with one more out, if he gets it.

Stephenson missed a curve, watched a called second strike, then took two balls. On the fifth pitch Jim wrapped a curve around the youngster's bat and the game—the perfect game, from top to bottom—was over.

That night it became official. Jim Bunning appeared as a special guest star on the Ed Sullivan Show, for a cool thousand dollars.

James Paul Bunning, out of Southgate, Kentucky, the same town that gave millionaire jockey Eddie Arcaro to the world, is now 33 years old. Last year was his tenth in the majors, but only his first season in the National League. For nine years, after a minor league apprenticeship in Richmond (Ohio-Indiana League), Davenport in the Three-Eye, Williamsport in the Eastern, Buffalo in the International, Little Rock in the Southern Association, and Charleston in the American Association, Jim had been the mainstay of the Detroit Tigers pitching staff.

In 1957, his third year in the big-time, Jim won 20 games for the Tigers, against 8 losses. If he could have won only one more game in '64, he would have emerged as that rarity—a pitcher with 20-game seasons in both leagues.

In all, Jim won 118 games for the Tigers and on two occasions he led all American League pitchers in the strikeout department. He pitched on five American League All-Star teams, with an impressive mark of four hits yielded in 14 innings.

By all odds his record in the American League had stamped him as one of the genuine pitching stars of his circuit. Yet a succession of Detroit managers were never quite satisfied with his work. For one thing, they felt Jim's temperament could stand a little mellowing. He was alternately rated a hot-head, by his own pilots, and a "head-hunter" by enemy batsmen.

However, nobody ever faulted his intelligence and serious devotion to the game. A stockbroker in the off-season, he represented the American League players in their pension demands.

The year Jim won 20 for the Tigers he gave up 33 home runs. In '63, his final season with Detroit, he won only 12 games, against 13 losses, and threw up 38 home run pitches, to lead all pitchers in the American League.

"I don't care how many homers I give up, if I win," said Jim. But the Detroit management had tired of his gopher problem. Their solution was to ship him out of the league in December, 1963. Lots of eyebrows were raised by the deal. The Phillies gave up Don Demeter, a prodigious RBI man, and minor league hurler Jack Hamilton, for Jim and Gus Triandos.

Those in the Detroit camp who had thought the 6' 3" graduate of Xavier University in Cincinnati was washed up, turned out to be sadly mistaken.

By All-Star time of 1964, Bunning was again chosen for the All-Star team. But this time it was the National

League club. He pitched two good innings for the Nationals and permitted two singles.

It was obvious the Phils had gotten just what they wanted, a leader for their improved pitching staff. As the Phils moved ahead in the race, Jim became the "stopper" and Mauch, who was playing in the American League when Bunning was a Tiger mainstay, insisted, "He's a better pitcher now because he has better control."

"Delivery, that's what Bunning has," said the Philly pilot. "He throws strikes now. Just check his record of walks. It's amazing."

Bunning, himself, thought he was making fewer mistakes than ever before. "I get the ball where I want it more consistently," he said. At season's end he'd given up only 46 walks in 284 innings and his strikeout total was still a bright 219. Jim is now eighth on the list of still-active pitchers in the strikeout department. He has 1,625 Ks on his ledger. The sportswriters voted him the NL's comeback player of the year in a post-season AP poll, but that didn't assuage Jim's feelings about the loss of the pennant.

Obviously Jim Bunning has improved over the years. In July, 1958, he pitched a no-hitter for the Tigers at Fenway Park over the Boston Red Sox. He had to throw 132 pitches to do it and two men walked. Six years later, pitching in the other league, he unfolded his perfect game.

If the man keeps on mellowing and learning, as he goes along, there's no telling what's ahead. Maybe a perfect game, with only 27 pitches.

25
JOHN BEAZLEY:
SPECIAL WAR VICTIM

Are professional baseball players men who play a boy's game? Or are they boys who never grow up? Read this article and decide what **you** think. It would be nice to say there was a happy ending to John Beazley's story, but the star of the 1942 World Series never made it back to the big leagues after joining the Dallas Eagles of the Texas League. One might say he was one of the minor casualties of World War II. But the events weren't minor to the right-handed pitcher who was the subject of Bill Rives' article from **The Dallas Morning News.**

By Bill Rives

You're a baseball pitcher. You've always been one, in your heart. Even as a kid in Nashville, you tried to throw the ball like the big guy on that good semipro team or those Southern Association pitchers. Sometimes, you'd sneak into the Nashville park and other times there'd be somebody who'd pay your way in. Those were your happiest moments, watching the pitcher fog those balls over the plate.

As you grew bigger, you began playing baseball on school teams. Naturally, you wanted to be a pitcher. So you pitch, and you're pretty good. One day, you read in the papers that the Cincinnati Reds are going to hold a baseball school in Nashville. Back in those days—fourteen years ago—kids had to pay their own way to the baseball schools. This one cost $15.

So you save fifteen bucks out of the money you make working around a drugstore and making deliveries on your bicycle. You go to this school and when it's over, you're signed up as a professional baseball player. That's the biggest moment of your life.

But you're green and raw and only sixteen years old, so you're shipped to a Class D league. You make sixty bucks a month. You begin the inevitable Odyssey of a rookie—first one club, then another. It's a tough game. Sometimes, you're hungry. Sometimes, you can't make the pitching staff. Sometimes, you get disgusted. You want to quit. But you know you can't. Baseball's in your blood. Good or bad, you're going to stick it out. Because you love it.

You're impatient. You've got your eyes on the big leagues but you don't know whether you can make it. But you keep plugging and you listen carefully to what wiser men have to say.

And gradually, as the months go by, as the months stretch into years, you improve. Finally, you're told one day, late in the 1941 season, you're going up to the big time. The St. Louis Cardinals want you. It's hard to believe and you swallow and blink your eyes and feel like a silly fool. But now, at the age of 22, you're going up.

A baseball career lies ahead of you in the major leagues. You're young and strong and smart and you can make that ball do tricks as it leaps toward the plate.

You go into your first full major league in 1942 and quickly you become a star. You win twenty-one games and lose only six. You help the St. Louis Cardinals to the National League pennant and you're hailed as one of the greatest pitching prospects in years.

In the World Series the Cardinals meet the New York Yankees. Your heart has never pumped so hard before as you take the mound in the second game. The Yankees won the first game and now you are expected to put the Cards back into the series. You recover quickly from your nervousness and the ball goes over the plate under full control. You're hot.

You win the game, 4 to 3, and the Cards keep rolling.

You win the fifth and final game, too, 4 to 2. The Cardinals, after losing the first game, sweep the next four. You're a world champion. You're riding high. You're at the top of your profession and you're in the big dough. The headlines with your name in them look good, too. You reflect how proud are the folks back home. Then you go into the service and one day, in 1944, you're asked to pitch for your service team. You're not in shape, but you can't turn down the guys you live with. So you pitch, and late in the game you know your arm is weak. But you don't complain, and play out the full nine. Afterward, under the shower, you can't raise your arm even with your shoulder. Your arm feels dead.

You're a little panicky at first. Your arm is your bread and butter. Your arm is what keeps you in baseball, and baseball is your life. Ah, it's nothing, you tell yourself. Just a sore arm. It will be all right tomorrow.

But tomorrow it isn't right. And that night and every other night, your right arm hurts like a toothache.

Still you tell yourself it's nothing to worry about. Those major league doctors know all about these arm troubles. They can fix you up.

When you get out of the service you go back to the Cardinals in 1946. But your confident belief that you can come back, that your arm can be made as good as new is shattered. You haven't got it any more, because you can't throw without having that sharp, shooting pain electrify your shoulder. Every time you throw a ball, you favor your arm. There's a hitch in your delivery and it ruins you.

You're sold in 1947, to the Boston Braves. One of their officials saw you in an exhibition game. You pitched the first few innings. Sometimes, your arm would hold together for a few innings. You happened to look pretty good that day. And so the Braves bought a lemon.

You've been to a lot of doctors and the Braves send you to more. But the wing is dead, just as dead as if it were buried like a dog's bone in the back yard.

So you're sold down to Nashville. You, a guy who won twenty-one games for the Cards in 1942 and pitched the

Redbirds to two World Series victories that same year, are now coming to the end of the trail. You've had only one good year in the major leagues.

At Nashville, someone tells you about a doctor, an orthopedic surgeon named Benjamin Fowler. Why don't you try him? Well, you're desperate and one more doc can't hurt. So you go to him. He studies your case for weeks and finally decides you've torn a capsule in your shoulder, a gristle-like substance that helps hold the arm to the shoulder. He operates on you—this is in May, 1948—and you're on the table for four hours and forty-five minutes. When it's over, he tapes your arm tightly to your side and tells you not to move it for several months. Not weeks, but months.

Finally, when the arm is free, you ease into your pitching. He has told you it will take a long time for your arm to heal. You report back to the Braves for 1949 spring training but you take things easy. You can't help them so they ask you to manage the St. Petersburg, Fla., farm team. But as a manager, you haven't the time to take care of your arm and so you throw in the towel after about six weeks.

Back to Nashville you go and you throw the ball on the sidelines and in batting practice. You get into only four games. You win one, a 3-hitter, and lose the other three.

But now another season is at hand. Your arm feels fine. You've been pitching in the Nashville YMCA and you haven't had a single pain.

One day you're told that you've been sold to the Dallas Eagles. Well, that's in the Texas League—a good place to get started back to the big leagues. You're thirty years old, almost thirty-one, and you figure you've got a few years left. It's hard to get rid of the reputation of being a "sore-armer," but you feel in your heart you can make it back to the majors.

So you get down to New Braunfels, Texas, and you drive out to the Mission Valley Guest Ranch. You look up Charley Grimm, the manager.

"I'm Johnny Beazley," you tell him. And Grimm, who

knows all about you and what's in your heart, sticks out a big paw and welcomes you to camp.

26
CASEY STENGEL: FILIBUSTER CHAMPION

One could fill an entire book with Casey Stengel stories. But if the book were limited to 10,000 pages, half of the good ones would be left out. Trying to interview Stengel was a test for any writer, because words flowed from the man's mouth with all the thrust of an ocean wave during a storm. Some say Stengel was overrated and contributed little to the success of the New York Yankees. Others say the downfall of the Yanks began when he was removed from the job as their manager. One thing on which all agree—he was one of the most colorful individuals in the history of the game.

By Arthur Daley

St. Petersburg, Fla.—"I ain' talkin'," said Charles Dillon Stengel. The Yankee manager folded his arms across his manly bosom and stared stonily across Miller Huggins Field, just like a sphinx. But soon his vocal cords began to simmer and seethe in the fashion of a volcano that has been suppressed too long. An eruption was inevitable.

"I'm kinder dead this year," was his feeble explanation. "I can't talk."

So the tourist merely sat in the dugout with him, waiting patiently for the hot, molten lava to come cascading forth. It was to be the Last Days of Pompeii, total engulfment.

"Now you can take Cerv," began Stengel for no particular reason at all. It wasn't surprising, though, because Ol' Case frequently starts his conversations in the middle.

"Like I wuz sayin', you can take Cerv and I'll explain it to you. At one time or another we had the three most valuable players in the American Association. One wuz Cerv, one wuz Skowron and one wuz Power, which I got rid of, and none of them did nuthin' the followin' season. But he can hit left-handed pitchin' and he can hit right-handed pitchin' and he can pinch-hit, a very handy feller to have on our ball club I don't mind sayin'."

There now will be a slight pause for station identification.

The last chap he was discussing was not Cerv or Skowron or Power but Enos Slaughter. How did Enos get into the discussion? Who knows?

"Now just look at that kid, Carter, on third," said the virtually mute manager. "He's gotta good arm. You can tell by the way he throws."

A tourist is bound to learn something if he listens long enough to the Ol' Perfessor. If a man throws well, he has a good arm. Betcha never knew that before.

"For the first time and I'd better knock wood on this," Stengel droned on, "Mantle comes to spring trainin' in good health and he's a first-class man in so many ways which he did like he got power, speed and an arm but strikes out too much. What's wrong with Bauer and it seems a lotta clubs desire him which you know and Noren had a very good year although I don't like to have a left-handed thrower in left field. Hey, Mantle, thatsa way to bunt you might hit .400 and beat Berra out."

The last sentence was shouted to Master Mickey after the erstwhile boy wonder had deftly dragged a bunt down the first-base line.

Stengel's roving eyes stopped at sight of a mob of ball players clustered near first base, all candidates for the job there. The leading candidate, at the moment, is Bill (Moose) Skowron, a reformed football player from Purdue and a powerful right-handed hitter.

"The reason Skowron stayed in the outfield his second year," said Casey, picking up a conversational thread from the tangle, "is that I delayed him. You can look it up but I think he led the American Association two years in hittin' although I may be wrong. Yankee success at first has been with lefty hitters but when you mention Gehrig you take in a lot of time.

"Mr. Kryhoski played on our ball club part of the year and he lives in New Jersey where a lotta writers and ball players live. He once hit sixteen home runs in the American League which ain't the American Association but the big leagues although he only hit one homer last year with Baltimore which is a bad ball park.

"He's thrilled to be back with the Yankees and one of the things which annoys the management is the salaries of all the first basemen we've got which is more than the rest of the league combined. We have the most first basemen, the largest and they eat the most which you should see their hotel bills.

"And now we come to Collins which may be an outfielder. He played center field in Newark and also played right field for me in the world series. You can look it up but he had Novikoff on one side of him and someone else whose name I've forgotten on the other but you can look it up. That should prove he's a great outfielder in order to be able to do it with them guys on either side of him.

"There's a kid infielder named Richardson who wuz in our rookie camp which he don't look like he can play because he's stiff as a stick but—whoost!—and the ball's there and he does it so fast it would take some of them Sunshine Park race track handicappers with the field glasses to see him do it so fast does he do it. He never misses. As soon as he misses a ball we'll send him home.

"We start out to get us a shortstop and now we got eight of them. We don't fool we don't. I ain't yet found a way to play more than one man in each position although we can shift them around and maybe make outfielders outa them or put 'em at ketch like we done with Howard but if some of the second division teams don't start beatin' Cleveland we may be in trouble.

"Like I said, though, I wanna see some of these guys before I start passin' comment and that's why I ain't talkin'."

Sorry, folks. That's why it's impossible to offer any quotes today from Charles Dillon Stengel, the sphinx of St. Pete.

27
ROBERTO CLEMENTE:
A FINAL LOOK

For years Roberto Clemente complained that he didn't receive the recognition he deserved. After breaking into the major leagues with the Pittsburgh Pirates in 1955, Clemente went on to lead the National League in hitting four times with batting averages ranging from .329 to .357. But Clemente was unhappy with his acclaim— or lack of it—when the Pirates went into the 1971 World Series. At the age of 37 the outfielder felt that Series might be his last chance for a national forum. He didn't waste the opportunity, hitting safely in all seven games and batting .414 with 12 hits in 29 at bats to lead Pittsburgh to its championship. Clemente at last received the accolades he desired.

But he was tragically correct about the 1971 Series being his last time in the national spotlight. Pittsburgh lost the league playoff in 1972. Then, on December 31 of that year, Clemente was killed in a plane crash one mile off the shore of Puerto Rico. He wasn't on his way to a baseball game. He was trying to bring relief supplies to earthquake victims in Nicaragua. In recognition of Clemente's greatness, the Baseball Writers of America voted to ignore their rule requiring that a player be inactive for five years before becoming eligible for the

Hall of Fame. Clemente was immediately placed with the immortals. It wasn't a difficult decision: At the end of his final season, Clemente had become the 11th player in baseball history to collect 3,000 hits. In 18 years with Pittsburgh, Clemente became their all-time leader in games (2,433), at bats (9,454), hits (3,000), singles (2,154) and total bases (4,492). He ranked among the all-time Top 10 in the National League for games, at bats, hits, singles and total bases. He was among the Top 20 in all five categories for all of baseball and had a .312 lifetime batting average. He also had won 12 Gold Gloves awards as an outfielder.

By Stan Hochman

Roberto Clemente turned the World Series into a mano-a-mano with Frank Robinson and then he won it from here to Barcelona. When it was over, Clemente earned two ears, a tail, four hooves, and a fancy-schmancy sports car, which is more than Manolete ever got. But then again, Manolete could not play right field the way Roberto Clemente can play right field. Nobody can play right field the way Roberto Clemente can.

"I proved nothing to myself," Clemente said yesterday after the Pirates had gutted out a 2–1 victory over Baltimore to win the whole wonderful tournament. "I know what I am capable of. But I proved lots of things to lots of other people."

They played out the drama in Baltimore's drab, lumpy, shabby Memorial Stadium. On Saturday, Clemente proved some more things to some more people when he tripled to left-center the very first time up.

"He was storming around the batting cage before the game," Brooks Robinson said afterward. "He had read that article about him not being able to pull the ball. He

---

was ranting about what he had to do to prove what kind of hitter he is."

It was a nerve-grinding 10-inning game and Clemente snuffed out one threat with a throw from the right field corner that crackled through the Maryland haze like a bolt of lightning. "It had to be the greatest throw I've ever seen," said Dave Johnson, who was standing at home plate at the time. "One moment he's got his back to the plate at the 309 mark and the next instant here comes this throw, on the chalk line."

But Saturday's bravos belonged to Robinson, who struggled through a hitless day. He walked in the 10th, rumbled from first to third on a single to center, beating the throw with a head-first slide. Then he raced home on Brooks Robinson's fly ball to medium-center, beating the throw that took a wicked high hop.

Sunday belonged to Clemente. He homered to left-center his second time up. That gave him 12 hits for the tournament. He wound up batting .412, with two homers and four runs batted in. He also wound up with a whole new outlook on life at age 37.

"I now have peace of mind," he said, solemn and hoarse in the euphoric babble of the Pittsburgh clubhouse. "All the years I have one regret, that the image of me that the writers write is not a true image.

"Always the sarcastic stories about my injuries. Never the fact that I still play, even when I'm hurt. I lead this club since I got here, but all you ever read is that I am grouchy, selfish, only for myself. Ask my teammates."

"For a superstar," pitching hero Steve Blass said, "he's one of the most approachable guys I've ever seen. He's a helluva easy guy to get along with. He plays the game harder than anybody I've ever seen. He plays so hard, he doesn't look graceful and that makes him exciting."

"Having him out there giving everything," said Willie Stargell, "makes you give everything. He's exciting. He doesn't play safe baseball."

"When I first came to the big leagues," Dave Cash said, "I didn't realize how great and how valuable he was. I can't find the adjectives to describe what he offers to the club, he's so great."

"He is the best all-around player today in baseball," said Jose Pagan. "He does everything for you. You never see him play slow. He always gives 150 percent of his body."

"He is," bubbled general manager Joe Brown, "the best player I have ever seen. I have never seen a player give more of himself. The writers who only wrote about the injuries overlooked the paramount factor, the way he produces."

Nobody else can run and throw and hit like Clemente can, but the sight of a 37-year-old man thrashing around the drab and lumpy ball park probably planted some ideas with his younger teammates.

Robinson, in a slightly less flamboyant way, has been leading by example for years. "I don't ask guys to slide head-first," he said softly. "I don't ask guys to stand as close to the plate as I do. But if it rubs off. . . . All I ask guys to do is give 100 percent on the field."

Robinson was on his way to a splendid series himself, until he got drilled in the hip by a Bruce Kison fast ball Wednesday night. The snap went out of his swing and he never got another hit after that.

He has an Achilles tendon that is tender and he yanked a hamstring muscle Saturday in that vital dash from first to third. You did not read a great deal about the injuries because that is not Robinson's style. How close to 100 percent was he for the seventh game?

"I was about 55 percent," he said glumly. "It wasn't that I felt I had to play. It's just that I wanted to play." If he hadn't gone 0-for-4 and if somebody else could have hammered out some clutch hits against Steve Blass and if Merv Rettemund had not bobbled Pagan's double for the instant that enabled Stargell to lumber home with the winning run, you might be reading a lot more about Robinson's leadership qualities today.

"Why does a team need a leader?" asked Bill Virdon, who is the next manager of the Pirates. "Walking to the plate, and getting a hit with a man on, that's leadership."

Clemente knows this too. "I told the team in August when I was out of the lineup," he recalled, "that I would carry them when I got back. It put pressure on me because then I had to do it."

Clemente did carry the team to a pennant, and through the playoffs and through the World Series, carrying them on those shoulders he was constantly twitching to ease the pain in his back. Nobody is snickering at him now and it is about time.

28
BROOKLYN, 1955:
REWARD FOR PATIENCE

Joe Trimble of the **New York Daily News** did a masterful job combining the past with the present when he put together this on-the-spot story after the Brooklyn Dodgers won the 1955 World Series. I remember catching bits and pieces of the game while undergoing basic training at Sampson Air Force Base, which like the Brooklyn Dodgers is no longer in operation. However, the man who managed the Dodgers that October afternoon is still very much in operation. He's Walter Alston, who managed the Dodgers in the 1974 Series against the Oakland A's. And many of the other individuals mentioned in the story are still active in the game. Phil Rizzuto has become a popular broadcaster for his former team, while Elston Howard completed his seventh year as a Yankee coach in 1974. Junior Gilliam became a coach for Alston in 1965. He was coaching at first base during the '74 Series and many felt he would become the Dodgers' next skipper. Gil Hodges went on to become the manager of the New York Mets, guided them to a world championship in 1969,

and then was struck down by a fatal heart
attack just before the 1972 season began. He
was succeeded by Yogi Berra, who was in the
losers' dressing room that day in 1955.

By Joe Trimble

They won't make October 4 a red-letter day in Brooklyn. They'll print it in letters of gold from now on because
it's only the greatest date in the history of the batty
borough—the day those darling Dodgers finally won the
World Series. At exactly 3:45 yesterday afternoon in the
Stadium, the Brooks got the final out of a 2-0 victory over
the Yankees in the seventh and deciding game.

And when they print calendars over there, they won't
bother with Marilyn Monroe's picture. Not good enough.
They'll have pucker-faced Johnny Podres, the most heroic
pitcher in Dodger-town since Dizzy Vance and the only
Brooklyn thrower ever to win two games in a Series. It
was Podres' brilliant, crushing pitching which ruined the
AL champions, sending them down to their fifth Series
loss in 21.

And who do you suppose knocked in both Brook runs?
No one else but Gil Hodges, the batting flop of the '52
Series.

There were many memorable events bright and tragic
on this earth on past 4ths of October, but the hallowed
pages of history must display yesterday's momentous
triumph above them all.

What kind of a date has it been? Well, on October 4,
1861, the Union forces massed to form the Army of the
Potomac; in 1864, the Erie Railroad opened (probably
not on time); in 1940, Hitler and Mussolini met at the
Brenner Pass and, in 1944, the U.S. Army broke through
the German West Wall. Al Smith, the beloved Governor
of New York and Presidential candidate, also died on the
latter date.

As far as Brooklyn is concerned, nothing ever could match the events of yesterday, when all the years of frustration and defeat were wiped out in one blazing afternoon. It was the 49th Dodger Series game in eight appearances, and the tightest, most tense and thrilling of them all.

At the finish, when Pee Wee Reese surehandedly threw out Elston Howard, the big park in the Bronx exploded with human emotion as the entire Dodger team raced out on the field and danced and drooled in delight around Podres.

While the 62,465 customers were cheering the new champs, the proud Yankees were filing slowly into the losing dressing room: a unique experience for them. Of all, only coaches Frank Crosetti and Bill Dickey and shortstop Phil Rizzuto had ever experienced a loss before. They had it but once, when the Cardinals smeared the Yankees four in a row after losing the 1942 opener.

The Dodgers are in paradise, finally succeeding after numerous Brooklyn teams had tried for four decades. The 1916 Flatbushers were knocked off by the Red Sox and the 1920 crew by Cleveland. Then the drought set in and it wasn't until 1941 that a pennant waved alongside the tree that grew in Brooklyn. But that year they had to play the Yankees, and Mickey Owen muffed a third strike and everything went black in the borough.

Four times since then, they won the NL flag only to find those merciless Yankees on the other side of the field—and the Brooks on the losing end of the playoff. They went down in 1947 in seven games, in 1949 it was five, in '52 seven again, and six in '53.

So the Brooks also went home with their heads hanging and the taunt of "Wait 'til next year!" shattering their eardrums. Now that's over. Next year came on October 4 this time.

This not alone was the greatest day in Brooklyn's history. It also brought to a wondrous climax the richest World Series ever. Due to increased admission prices and the maximum number of games, the $2,337,515.34 taken in at the box office is an all-time high.

Numerous records were set, but the one the Brooklyn players will remember most was their achievement in winning four of the last five games after dropping the first two. This kind of comeback had never happened in a seven-game Series before.

To do it, they had to get a second superior pitching job from the 23-year-old Podres, their little left-hander, and also they had to whip the Yankee pitcher who had given them the most trouble, 35-year-old Tommy Byrne. Although they got only three hits off the graying southpaw before an error helped cause his removal in the sixth, they put them in exactly the right places.

Roy Campanella, who had gone hitless in 12 times up in the Stadium this Series and had a lifetime average of .070 in the big park, crashed a double to left after one out in the fourth. Duke Snider, who went all the way on his bad knee, fanned just before Campy's hit. Carl Furillo followed with a slow grounder, Rizzuto making a fine play to get him at first as Campy reached third. Gil Hodges, with a count of one ball and two strikes, swung at an inside curve. He didn't get much wood on the ball but it went safely to left field and the Brooks were ahead.

The other safety was a lead-off single in the sixth by Reese, the veteran whose victory appetite was greatest because it had been on the losing side against the Yankees five times.

The shortstop lined a hit to left-center and was deprived of a double when Bob Cerv made a fine retrieve. Reese eventually scored the insurance run after Bob Grim had taken the mound.

But before the Brooks opened the thin gap, they nearly gave the Yankees a run. Yogi Berra opened the bottom of the fourth with a lazy fly to center, a bit to Snider's right. Junior Gilliam came over from left, invaded the Duke's realm, and then they went into an Alphonse-Gaston act. The ball tipped off Snider's glove as he made a last-second grab after realizing Gilliam was letting him take it. That fluke double gave Berra the distinction of being the ninth man ever to hit safely in every game of a full-length

Series. The catcher made ten hits, topping the batters on both sides.

The Yankee fans screamed for blood after the break. It's an old axiom that you can't make a mistake against the Bombers. They break through the opening and kill you. But Podres wouldn't buckle. He got the next three batters, all strong righty sluggers. Hank Bauer hit a fly to Furillo, Bill Skowron grounded to Don Zimmer, and Cerv popped to Reese in short left. The Dodger fans screamed: "Pee Wee! Pee Wee!" as he went out and Gilliam came in and the Dodger captain caught it.

The Yankee supporters applauded Gilliam when he came up to bat in the fifth, one guy screaming: "He's the best man we've got!" Junior didn't get a chance to flub anything else in the outfield because he was moved in to second base after the Brooks got their run in the sixth.

After Reese hit, Snider bunted deftly along the third-base line. Byrne fielded it and threw accurately to first base. Skowron stepped forward to meet the ball, taking his foot off the bag and forcing himself to make a tag play. He swiped at the Dodger runner's back and the ball flew out of his glove for an error.

Walter Alston, winning a World Series in his first try, sensibly ordered Campy to sacrifice and he did. Byrne handled this bunt, too. It seemed that the pitcher had a force possibility on Reese at third, Pee Wee not yet having gone into a belly-whop slide. But Byrne thought otherwise and let Reese make it, tossing to first for the out. Casey Stengel ordered an intentional pass to Furillo and then called in Grim, his relief ace who had saved the first game but was battered as starter in the fifth.

Grim's first batter was Hodges, a tough man with the bases filled. Gil took a strike and then drove a long sacrifice fly to center, Reese scoring. Grim walked Hoak, refilling the lanes, but got George Shuba, a pinch-hitter for Zimmer, on a third-out grounder.

Again the sight of a Dodger run on the scoreboard brought a Yankee threat in the bottom of the inning. This developed into a real big one and also produced the greatest fielding play of the Series—a catch by Sandy

Amoros, an outfielder who was held lightly as a prospective regular in the spring because of his shabby fielding and throwing.

Podres, who passed only two, hit a wild streak and walked Billy Martin on four straight pitches. Alston came out to give the youngster a chance to get his breath. With victory so close, he didn't want the kid to get hysterical. Johnny threw two bad pitches to McDougald, then got one over, which Gil bunted perfectly for a single, Martin taking second.

Then came the key play, the one which probably meant the title. Stengel, disdaining a bunt with Berra up, had Yogi swing away. Podres pitched outside and Berra stroked a long, high fly into the left-field corner. Amoros, playing him far over toward center, had to run over 100 feet. The ball stayed up a long time, being held by the wind, and Sandy just reached it, gloving it with his right mitt in fair territory.

Martin and McDougald, not believing a catch possible, were on their horses. Billy suddenly reversed himself when almost to third and Gil was past second base before he found out the ball had been held. Amoros gracefully whirled and fired to Reese, who went into short left for the throw. Pee Wee then made another perfect throw to Hodges, just getting McDougald as he slid back. That was the 12th Brooklyn DP, a new Series record.

Bauer then hit a hopper to short and Reese couldn't get it out of his glove for a frantic portion of a second. When he did, he had to throw a blazer and it just beat the runner, according to first-base umpire Frank Dascoli.

Grim was lifted for a pinch-hitter in the seventh, after Howard singled. There were two out, so Stengel sent up his hobbled husky, Mickey Mantle. Podres fooled the Mick with a change-up, Mantle skying the ball to short left where Reese took it, with the Dodger fans again screaming his name.

Podres had a rough time in the eighth, when the Yankees got their second runner to third base. Rizzuto led off with a single to left but Martin flied to Furillo, who came in fast for the looper. McDougald then hit a sharp grounder which bad-hopped off the left arm of Don Hoak, playing third because Jackie Robinson had a sore Achilles tendon in his right foot. Rizzuto got to third as the fluke hit went into left.

The tension was terrific, with Berra and Bauer coming up. Podres really had it, getting Berra to cut under one of his slow curves. The ball went to Furillo in short right and Carl gunned it home, holding The Scooter on third. Then the youngster faced his supreme test in Bauer, who hits left-handers very well. He took Hank to 2-2 with curves and slow-up pitches, then flung himself off the mound by putting all he could on a shoulder-high fastball which Bauer swung at and missed.

As the Yanks came up, Dodger fans stayed seated. Yankee adherents shouted for a rally.

Skowron cracked a sizzler back to Podres, the hard grounder sticking in his glove web. He was unable to get it out for a second or so, and started to run toward first base to make the putout that way. But he was able to pry it loose and make an underhand toss to Hodges. Cerv then hit a high fly which Amoros took in short left and the Dodgers were one out away from the promised land.

Podres went to 2-2 on Howard and then made him swing off stride at the change-up. Reese took one happy step toward the grounder, aimed it for Hodges, and, though the toss was a bit low, Gil kept his foot on the base and the Dodgers had finally arrived in paradise.

29
CARL YASTRZEMSKI: TROUBLED SUPERSTAR

Fenway Park in Boston has one of the smaller seating capacities in major-league baseball. But the fans who go through its turnstiles are among the fanatics of baseball. With the decline of the New York Yankees Fenway partisans saw their team become a strong con-

tender, and each spring their hopes for a
championship were high. However, except in
1967, those hopes would fade as the leaves
started falling from the trees near the Charles
River in Boston. Managers and players came
and went in a revolving door atmosphere, and
the Red Sox had plenty of heated controversy,
much like the successful Oakland A's. Some
say the reason for that controversy was Carl
Yastrzemski. This story by Ray Fitzgerald gives
some insight into the problems of being a
superstar named Yaz.

By Ray Fitzgerald

The Red Sox gathered up their gloves and other equipment and straggled into the tunnel that led to the dressing
room under Tiger Stadium that night last October, and
you wondered how hard they would take the defeat.

The championship had just been snatched out of their
hands. They'd beaten the Orioles two out of three and
had come roaring into Detroit knowing that another two
out of three over the Tigers would give them the Eastern
Division title in the American League.

The Red Sox were going to have to gamble with rookie
lefthander John Curtis against Mickey Lolich in the first
game, but after that they could go with Luis Tiant, who
had been practically perfect the last two months. Ace
Marty Pattin was ready for the final game of the season.

And Curtis might have won for them, except that Luis
Aparicio slipped coming from third to home on a Carl
Yastrzemski blast. The two were hung up on third base
and Aparicio was tagged out. A possible big inning
brought nothing and the Red Sox lost, 4-1.

Tiant was brilliant the next night, but again the Red
Sox didn't hit. Yastrzemski, Reggie Smith, Carlton Fisk,

Rico Petrocelli, Tommy Harper—the bats that had carried the team into the stretch run were silent against Woody Fryman, and the Tigers prevailed, 3-1.

Now, I had seen losing clubhouses before in big games, in Super Bowls, seventh games of World Series. I saw the Lakers lose to the Celtics in an NBA final that should have been theirs, when the victory party with the champagne and the big balloons were ready to roll.

I'd talked to golfers who had blown thousands of dollars by missing a two-foot putt. The point is, I had seen the misery of final defeat in a sports event, the funereal air that pervades a locker room when there are none of those tomorrows the broadcasters are always talking about.

But I wasn't ready for the Red Sox clubhouse five minutes after Al Kaline had gloved Ben Oglivie's fly ball for the final out. Don't forget, this was the team called the Country Club A.C. Nobody had ever confused the Red Sox with the Three Musketeers' "one for all, all for one" motto.

After the Fisk-Smith-Yastrzemski "non-hustling" incident in mid-1972, another club had mockingly dubbed the Red Sox "Unity University."

All this did not jibe with the atmosphere in the Boston locker room that night in Detroit. Many veterans were crying. Fisk, the brilliant rookie catcher who had only one RBI in the last three weeks, was inconsolable. Tommy Harper, who had played on losers all his life, couldn't find the words needed to describe his feelings at being deprived of being part of a winner.

And the one who took it hardest was the man the Fenway Park fans had been riding all year, the one they'd been saying didn't care because he had his three-year contract at $165,000 per, the one they had called the fat cat.

Carl Yastrzemski sat at his locker with the tears streaming down his cheeks as owner Tom Yawkey—who had made his first regular-season road trip since the '40s—tried to console him.

"You did your best," he told Yastrzemski. "You have nothing to be ashamed of."

"We let you down. We let ourselves down," replied Yastrzemski. "We should have won it."

The sting of that defeat has stayed with the Red Sox star through the winter.

"It was the biggest disappointment of my life," he said before heading for spring training in Winter Haven this year.

"Bigger than 1970, when you lost the batting title to Alex Johnston on the last day?" he was asked.

"No comparison," replied Yastrzemski.

But time wounds all heels, or whatever that expression is, and Yastrzemski heads into the 1973 season convinced that the Red Sox are a better team for what happened to them last year.

He has always been an optimist, anyway, and every spring is convinced the pitfalls of other years will be avoided, that the ones who hit .230 last season will hit .320 this year, that the 10-game winners will find 10 more wins somewhere.

Yastrzemski knows as well as anyone else in baseball-daffy Boston the reason the Red Sox didn't win in 1972.

It wasn't those two games with the Tigers, it was the first 75 games of the season when the team often played as though it would have trouble beating The Little Sisters of The Poor.

"That's when we lost it, in the first two months of the season. The guys really didn't believe in themselves until after July. We kept saying, 'Well, the Orioles will start coming any day now.' But they didn't, and neither did we."

In the last half of the season, though, the Red Sox had the best record in the league. The confidence began building then and it's still building.

There is no doubt the strike hurt the Red Sox, although that is copping a plea, because the strike hurt baseball in general. Smith, for one example, was playing brilliantly in spring training and had worked himself into peak form for the start of the season.

The came the strike. Smith was back where he started and only in flashes did he contribute the way he had in previous years.

But the big onus was on Yastrzemski. Every team has the big guy, the one who must do it, and with the Red Sox, Yaz has been the man ever since Ted Williams packed it in over a decade ago.

Last year, Yastrzemski was a colossal disappointment, at least in that first half of the season he pinpointed as the reason the Red Sox didn't win.

In Boston's first 15 games, Yastrzemski hit a whopping .164. Then he was hurt sliding home against the Angels and missed 26 games in which the Red Sox went 13-13.

He came back and went into a hot streak (46 for 126) that boosted his average to .314. He didn't look like the Yastrzemski of old because there were no homers in the output, but the surge was promising.

Unfortunately, it didn't last. In July, he went back into the doldrums, along with his team. He didn't hit a home run until July 22.

Actually the slump was a continuation of one that had begun in the last couple of months of 1971. Yastrzemski, always a controversial figure in Boston, was booed as though he was a Don Buddin, the butterfingered shortstop of a slightly earlier day.

Yaz reacted one night after a particularly bad outing by making a gesture of disgust (not obscene) at the crowd. This did not make things any easier for him.

A reporter went through the stands one day asking fans why they booed more when Yastrzemski struck out than when, say, Doug Griffin fanned.

The answer, as it usually is in sports these days, was money.

The thought that a man getting $165,000 wasn't hitting homers and driving in runs at a phenomenal rate grated on people, and was rationized into "He ain't tryin', what does he care, he got his dough in the bank."

But Yastrzemski, whatever his faults, does care. He always did, and that has always been a large part of the trouble. He is so intense, so impatient with failure, that it drives him to even greater determination to succeed. Sometimes this works—check out the record book for 1967—and sometimes it doesn't work.

Yastrzemski experiments with his swing when things go bad, something good hitters aren't supposed to do. Close the stance, open it, drop the left shoulder, hold the bat higher, meet the ball, take the first pitch.

He has tried them all.

Early last year, after a couple of Texas Ranger pitchers had made Yastrzemski look like Charlie Chaplin at bat, he conducted a midnight clinic in his hotel room.

He brought a bat back from Arlington Stadium and had Smith and Petrocelli check his swing. He watched himself in the mirror. For a couple of hours this went on and he announced he'd found the trouble.

But he hadn't, because except for those few weeks when he sprayed singles around the ball park, he stayed mired in a slump until almost September. At the end of July he was batting .262 and by Aug. 19 he had hit a low of .243.

The slump, almost a year old, bothered him so much he had just about decided it was his last season.

"I came within an inch of retiring. No, not in the middle of a season, I could never do that, but I figured I'd had it as a hitter and I just wasn't going to stay in baseball.

"It wasn't the riding from the fans that bothered me. Sure I didn't like it. My mother and father and wife and kids would go to the game and hear all the things people said. It's no fun to know your family is listening to all that. But I had begun to doubt my ability. I couldn't even hit in batting practice."

Then, one off-day, playing golf at home, he was smashing the ball off the tee and realized he still had the strength and timing.

Therefore, he concluded, the trouble must be mental. He was being defensive at bat and his concentration was tangled like spaghetti.

"Up until then, against lefties like Lolich and McNally, I was just trying to meet the ball. From that day on, I tried to attack it."

Enough of the old Yastrzemski came back to start the optimistic juices flowing again. Eight of his 12 homers for 1972 came during the September run, when the pressure was on. He hit .300 in September and drove in 25 runs.

His homer and RBI totals were both only one less than in September of 1967, when he was the one-man hitting gang that triggered The Impossible Dream.

So now there is no talk of retiring. Yastrzemski is 33, and to show how time flies, of the 40 men on the Red Sox training roster in his rookie season—1961—only one, Wilbur Wood of the White Sox, is still in the major leagues.

But Yastrzemski is a young 33. He has a strong, muscular body, and though there is a thickening around the middle that wasn't there 10, or even five years ago, he is too proud an athlete to let himself get out of shape.

"I'd like to play five to seven years more," he said this winter. To stay in shape for that sort of future, he went back to Gene Berde, the man who had helped him during the 40-homer years.

Berde is a physical education instructor at The Colonial Country Club in Lynnfield, the town Yastrzemski now calls home.

Yastrzemski had gone through the Berde torture chamber before the 1969 season, enduring a set of exercises that would make a strong man out of Tiny Tim.

When spring training began, his bat was as light as a toothpick. Running bases was a walk in the sun after what Berde had put him through.

Yaz hit .329 that season, losing out to Johnston for the batting title by less than a point. He smashed 40 homers, drove in 102 runs and played in 161 games.

Yastrzemski skipped the exercise routine the next winter, feeling that he was getting older and the routine might shorten his career.

He hit only .254 in 1971 with just 15 homers. But he stayed away from Berde the next winter too, and the final figures for 1972 were a .264 batting average, 68 runs batted in, and only 12 homers, lowest total since his rookie season.

"I thought I could take up the exercise slack by playing tennis," he said, "but that wasn't enough, so I've gone back to Gene. He busted my back but I've stayed with it."

Yastrzemski went to Winter Haven in mid-January, but he brought Berde's routine with him. In spring training, he also planned to spend more time in the batting cage, working with the hand exercises and using the heavy bat against the heavy rubber stand.

"I want to hit until my hands are red," he said before departing for Winter Haven.

So Yaz says he's ready, but let's get one thing straight. Carl Yastrzemski is no leader, in the Hollywood "let's go get 'em gang" sense of the word.

He is no Pete Rose, no holler guy. He would sooner fall off the Mystic River bridge than preside over a Kangaroo Court, the gimmick that Frank Robinson conducted to make the Orioles "a family" a few years ago.

The Red Sox star does not inspire his team by rhetoric. He doesn't go around the locker room whooping it up before games. You couldn't characterize him as a loner, but neither is he one of the guys.

Carl Yastrzemski, to tell the truth, is basically shy and other players find it hard to warm up to him. He has friends—Smith, Griffin and the departed Gary Peters were his closest in '72—but he'd never win a popularity contest.

"I've never been a leader," Yastrzemski said late last season, probably for the 100th time. "Why should I have to go around before each game getting guys up for it? This is a club of 25 professionals. They know what it's all about."

Billy Herman made Yastrzemski the captain back in 1966. It didn't last long, not because Yaz did anything wrong, but because he felt uncomfortable with the title, even though being captain of a baseball team is 99 & 44/100ths per cent honorary. You don't even get to call the coin flip.

If Yastrzemski is a leader, it is strictly inside the white lines and in the weekly statistics. He was a leader in 1967 because every time you looked up he was knocking in a run or making a great defensive play. Yastrzemski leads by example and the example the last couple of years has been less than ordinary.

Yastrzemski didn't get into much controversy in 1972. There was the thing when Carlton Fisk talked about "lack of leadership from veteran players," translated in the headlines to "lack of hustle." But the fuss didn't last long and Yastrzemski says he bears no animosity toward the plain-speaking young catcher.

"He told me he didn't say it the way it came out," said Yastrzemski, "and that's good enough for me."

He's been accused of interfering with managers, of talking behind their backs to Yawkey about them. He vehemently denies that, and since the arrival of Eddie Kasko, the charge has simmered down.

Yastrzemski has always praised Kasko in Eddie's three years in command. When Kasko was given a new two-year contract, Yastrzemski said, "That's good news. Some of the people on this club had better shape up, because Eddie Kasko has his seat planted in this dressing room for some time to come and the men should realize it."

Yaz said Kasko has made great strides as a manager.

"In the last half of the season I never saw him react in such positive fashion. You just didn't question the moves he made."

What about 1973? Do the Red Sox have enough to win it?

"Our pitching," said Yastrzemski, "is as good as any. Reggie [.270] and Rico [.240, 15 homers] need better years and they've shown they can produce."

Yastrzemski thought the Red Sox might trade for another power hitter at the winter meetings, because Boston doesn't have a true clean-up man.

Yaz has always batted third, and last season both Smith and Petrocelli were so-so in the fourth spot.

But general manager Dick O'Connell came home from Hawaii empty-handed. A couple of months later, however, after the designated hitter rule was passed, O'Connell signed Orlando Cepeda, aching knees and all, in the hope that Cepeda still had some of the power that has accounted for 357 homers in the National League.

If Cepeda can cut it, he would be a natural fourth hitter in Fenway Park.

Yastrzemski wants to play first base, but said Kasko's the boss, and if the boss says go back to left field, so be it.

First base, said Carl, keeps a man in the game, keeps

him on his toes. Yaz, an exceptional athlete, played well there last season. Whether he will return depends on many things—whether Cepeda can play regularly, whether rookie Dwight Evans makes it in the Red Sox outfield, whether Ben Oglivie is good enough to be a regular.

This is a crucial year for Yastrzemski. He's tasted the delights of superstardom and walked in the ashes of failure, and the critics that prowl the ancient ballyard on Jersey Street are waiting.

He has to prove to them he's back to a reasonable facsimile of what he was in 1967, when you and I were young and the world was his oyster.

It won't be easy, but you can't say Carl Yastrzemski isn't giving it his best.

30
DUSTY RHODES AND JOHNNY PODRES: FAME CAN BE BRIEF

Where are the summer flowers when December snows fall? What happens to yesterday's heroes? The late Jimmy Cannon, for two decades one of America's most talented sportswriters, provides an answer in this piece written in January of 1956.

By Jimmy Cannon

It was strictly a gimmick but it busted for space. The famous petits fours, which are, of course, high-class cookies, were supposed to name the guys they'd leap at during leap year. Run down the list and you see guys such as Sinatra, Brando, DiMaggio, Ty Power. It figures and so does Johnny Podres. The kid grabbed a hot hand. They're giving him the treatment since he beat the Yanks two games in the World Series.

All guys with hot hands get the ride until the straights stop filling in the middle. The cold wind blows away the aces, and deuces are in the hole. Bet the hot hand before the cold wind freezes your fingers. Some guys never run out of it. They stay lucky forever. Luck comes and holds. So, Johnny, take the plaques and deliver your talks at the banquets. Stand up there and let the television cameras inspect your kisser.

Some guys don't just get cold. They get lost and mixed up because they can't understand what happened. It was there, now it's gone. He's 1A now. So who knows? No one can measure how much a hot hand wins. It's table stakes and beyond that there's no limit at all.

You take Dusty Rhodes. He sizzled in '54. Cleveland couldn't get him out. Step down, Monte Irvin, Dusty Rhodes is hitting for you. And the Giants won in four straight. It runs the same way. They had parades in Rhodes' home town, too, back in Alabama. The mayor talked, just like the mayor of Witherbee, N.Y., when Podres went back where he came from.

It was hotter because Rhodes had Leo Durocher going for him. Two guys, Willie Mays and Dusty Rhodes, the manager spoke about that winter. He entertained a lot of people telling them what a big cut Dusty took at the bourbon. Everyone laughed. You're hot, everything's funny.

They didn't sit Dusty in an open car and take him down the big street back down in Alabama this October. Next thing he was in the papers getting banged up in an auto accident. But Ed Sullivan wasn't demanding his presence. Television got along very well without Dusty Rhodes. This was the winter they took the shot with Podres who held a hot hand against the Yankees.

Where's Durocher? Did you ever think he'd get chilly? One year the pennant, the next Durocher is out of baseball. He was allowed to quit a job he didn't hold. Don't worry about him. He can come back when he wants to.

The money will be right, too. I don't know where he'll light but a lot of clubs will take a shot with him. He's a big name. But it didn't help him on that television show. Did it? You ever see a colder man?

Often when I see Pee Wee Reese I think of the kid who came up with him. It turns across my mind that Pete Reiser led the National League in batting the first year he landed. No one ever did that before, or since. But he ran into a fence the next season. That was the end of it. It didn't just stop right there. He lasted but the greatness was lost and he hurt all over. And then he was being traded. And then he was gone.

Dizzy Dean stayed warm, long after his arm lost it. But he had won 30 and that's in the book. He's a talker and a comedian and he works at broadcasting and hollers up a loud commotion. But I remember when he should have been right, pitching for the Cubs against the Yankees in a World Series. The fog was off the fast ball. The curve didn't jump. And he tried to sneak by on con but he didn't make it. But that's another tale. He didn't stick around as long as some. But while he was up, they all knew about it. He played the hot hand the way it should be handled. He's still pulling high hole cards.

Once he was a hell of a fighter and he was loaded with money. The horses took it. The broads trimmed him. The joints got a lot of it.

And then doctors told him it would be hazardous for him to fight any more. They picked up his ticket and he owed last month's room rent. I met him at the gym one afternoon.

"Help me get a license," he said.

"You're liable to be hurt," I said.

"Naw," he said. "They got it in for me. Nothing wrong with me. I'm as good as ever."

They told him how bad it could be. Punches around the head could kill him or set him crazy. He's fine now but he's willing to take a chance. That's what it means to be hot. There's one guy willing to die for it.

You do, or you don't. It's not that simple. Lew Jenkins, when he was lightweight champion of the world, never

believed it at all. It was money and money was made
to spend and the hell with it all. Out of the Army, originally
a blacksmith, Jenkins is back in it again. He's a para-
trooper now. I never heard him complain. But years afterwards he was fighting for small purses and money was
money. He wanted it then.

"When you got a kid," Jenkins said, "it makes a difference."

Anyway, Nancy Berg and the other petits fours held
still for this gag about leaping at Johnny Podres. The press
agent didn't bother with Dusty Rhodes. He held the hot
hand in '54 and that's a century ago when a guy's shooting
angles to grab some space. The hot hand's Johnny's until
there's a new deal.

31
DON NEWCOMBE:
AN UNHAPPY TRIP HOME

It's fun to be a winner, but for every winner
there is a loser on the other side. This is a story
of the pitcher who lost the dramatic seventh
game of the 1956 World Series. It was a sad
ending to a season in which Don Newcombe
compiled a 27-7 record and earned the Cy
Young Award as his league's top pitcher. The
story, written by the late Milton Gross, is unique
because it developed as the sportswriter rode
home with Newcombe while the game was still
in progress.

By Milton Gross

It is only 35 miles and 70 minutes between Ebbets Field
and Colonia, N.J., but for Don Newcombe it was a life-

---

time. This was his longest voyage home and he wept all the way.

He drove his Ford station wagon with his right hand and with his left he held a handkerchief to his face. Sometimes he put it to his mouth, sometimes to his eyes and sometimes he dropped it on the seat between his legs. He balled it into his fist or he rolled it between his fingers and always he stared straight ahead, almost unseeing, because there was a mist before his eyes and memories he cannot erase.

Only Newcombe knew the gnawing pain within him, the doubts, the anger, the confusion and frustration of the pitcher who was reached for two home runs by Yogi Berra and one by Elston Howard, which beat the Dodgers yesterday.

But it was more than the game and the Series that went with it, more than being KO'd by the Yankees twice within a week and five times in a career. It was so much more than the conviction that he had good stuff and threw hard and courageously. It was a man being torn apart worse inwardly than he was on the field by forces beyond his control. It was a giant of a man, who needed the comforting of a child.

"It's tough, Newk," said a guy standing in the parking lot as we came to Don's car, "but you can't win them all."

Last week Newcombe hit a man who needled him as he entered his car, but this time the words didn't seem to touch him.

"I'm sorry, pop," Don mumbled as we drove away.

His voice was so low, his father couldn't hear.

"What?" he asked.

"I'm sorry," Don repeated.

"What have you got to be sorry for?" James Newcombe said to his son.

What, indeed? What could Newcombe say or what could his father say? And what are they all saying today? That he doesn't win the big ones . . . that he chokes when it's touch . . . that he showered hurriedly and left the field as quickly as he could after being replaced in the fourth and left his teammates to their despair.

It was all there in the car as we drove along Washington,

Flatbush and Atlantic Avenues, over the Manhattan Bridge, through the Holland Tunnel and along the Pulaski Skyway. It was all unsaid and hanging heavy in the air like the load that's within Don.

"How do I get rid of it?" he seemed to be thinking. "How do I get it out of my mind? How do I stop them from thinking that?"

As a newspaperman I was intruding in a time that should have been private, but I wanted to help. I didn't have the answers, but I had compassion.

"You won 27," I said. "You know there were some big ones among them."

"Remember that," Don's father said.

"I don't want to talk," Don said. "I don't want to say anything."

So we drove along in silence, a father and a son and an outsider, who had left a World Series game before it was done for the first time in 20 years.

"Don't you want to turn the game on the radio?" I asked Don.

"Not now," he said. "Not yet."

We were at Mulberry and Broome Sts. in Manhattan when Newcombe turned on the radio. Announcer Bob Wolf's voice was saying: "After six innings it's Yanks 5, Dodgers 0. Roger Craig now takes over the mound."

Newcombe listened, but seemed not to be listening. Twice he had to apply his brakes swiftly when his car came up on another too suddenly.

As we entered the Holland Tunnel, Billy Martin was at bat for the Yankees in the seventh, with one ball called.

The radio died under the river. "Why didn't you change your shirt and go back into the dugout?" I asked Newk because Manager Walter Alston instituted a rule last year after the Yankees KO'd Don in the opening game of the World Series that players must not leave the park before a game's completion.

"I don't know," he said. "I don't know a lot of things."

Approaching the New Jersey side, Newcombe compressed his lips. "I felt good," he said. "I was throwing hard, real hard."

The radio came alive again as we left the tunnel and Mickey Mantle walked in the seventh. "This brings up Yogi Berra with no out," Wolf said. "He has had two two-run homers and there's two aboard." There was a wild pitch, Martin going to third and Mantle to second.

"They're putting Berra on intentionally," the radio voice said, and his was the only sound in the car.

Bill Skowron was at bat. The cars whizzed by on the Pulaski Skyway. The Jersey meadows were barren and wind whipped the bulrushes when Skowron smashed his home run.

"It can happen to somebody else, too," Mr. Newcombe said, and Don merely nodded his head.

When Ed Roebuck came in and the announcer said he was Brooklyn's fourth pitcher, Don still seemed impassive. The fingers of his left hand rubbed the handkerchief he held and what was in his mind he didn't say until we left the skyway.

"In the second," he said, "after I had two and oh on (Johnny) Kucks, Jackie (Robinson) came over and asked if I was aiming the ball. I said I didn't think so."

Again we rode along in silence before I started to ask a question.

"I was getting the ball where I wanted it to go," Don said. "Except the first one Yogi hit."

"The first one," Newk said. "I tried to brush him back, but I didn't get it inside enough. When I came up in the third inning after Yogi hit the second one, he said to me: 'I hit a perfect pitch. It was perfect—low outside fast ball and I hit the hell out of it.' Mantle may hit more, but I respect Berra more. You can strike Mantle out, but I don't know where you can throw the ball to get Berra out."

"What about our hitters?" Mr. Newcombe said. "No hits the other day, two hits yesterday and what have they got today?"

"How do you figure that Stengel?" Newk asked. "Today against me he throws in all right-handers. The way Collins hits me, too. I don't understand it. I don't know about Slaughter, but why did he take Collins out the way he hits me?"

We were outside Linden then. "Drop me off at the house," Mr. Newcombe said, and Don nodded.

Norman, the youngest of Don's four brothers, answered the ring. "Too bad, Don," he said.

In the little parlor, the TV set was still on the game, but Newk's mother was in the kitchen. "Get it over with," she said. "It's over and done."

"I'm sorry, Ma," Newk said.

"What's to be sorry," she answered.

"A couple of guys I'll have to handle tomorrow," Norman said.

Newk went to the refrigerator for two quarts of beer and poured a glass for his dad, himself and me. "Drink up," he said. "I want to call my wife."

It was the ninth inning.

"You going to work tomorrow?" Newcombe's mother asked her husband.

"I don't think so," he said.

"Why worry about it. If it happened, it happened," she said.

"No hits. No hits at all," Don's brother said. "All of a sudden nobody hits. I'm biting my nails. Look at them."

Newk came back from his phone call. "Freddy was ironing and watching the game," he said. "She said it's all right. She asked when I was coming home."

When we were on the way, I asked Newk what he had been thinking about during the entire ride.

"I was thinking about what I do wrong," he said, "but I can't put my finger on why I do it. It always happens to me in the first two innings or the last."

For a moment Newk sat silent again. "I was running in the outfield at the Stadium the other day and a guy called me a yellow-bellied slob. How do you take things like that?" Newk said, with anguish.

"Today," Newk said, "before the game, Pee Wee (Reese) said: 'I don't care what you do today. We wouldn't be here without you.'"

"And other people say I choke up," Newk said, in a voice hoarse with emotion. "I think it's rubbed off in the clubhouse."

Ahead, I could see the Pennsylvania Railroad. I had told Newcombe I'd go home with him.

"I got to pass the railroad," he said.

I sensed he didn't want me coming with him all the way, at least not this day.

"How did you sleep last night?" I asked.

"Terrible," he said. "I was up four times. I took a pill but I couldn't sleep. I told my wife what's the use keeping you awake. She said for me to go in the other room, but I tossed and turned. It wasn't today's game. It was this other business I wanted to beat, but dammit, I can't get away from it."

We were at East Milton and Fulton in Rahway when I got out of the car. My sympathy was with this tormented man, who would give his soul to prove the big ones are like the little ones. There were five boys on the corner—four Negro and one white—and they recognized Newcombe as he drove off.

"That Newk?" one asked.

"How'd he get here so soon?" another said. "The game just ended."

"He left early," I said, and the white boy giggled.

"Don't laugh," one of the Negro boys said. "Just don't laugh."

32
KEN MCMULLEN:
A HUMAN BEING

In the day-to-day development of a major-league baseball season, one becomes very involved in the on-the-field accomplishments of the athletes. Baseball players seem to be either heroes or villains; there's a tendency to forget they are human beings, just like the fans, with real-life problems. Here's an in-depth look at the special troubles experienced by a member of the Los Angeles Dodgers while his team was moving toward the National League championship in 1974.

By Maury Allen

He will not get into a playoff game. He will not get into a World Series. He plays only one position, third base, and one of the best young Dodgers, Ron Cey, owns the territory.

Ken McMullen is 32. His curly black hair is thinning. His eyes are tired and his face is fleshy. He is no longer the bright young Dodger prospect of ten years ago or the big hitter for Gil Hodges and the Washington Senators or a regular for the Angels.

"After everything I've been through," he said, "worrying about playing regularly hardly seems important."

A year ago last May, McMullen's wife, Bobbie, went for a routine medical examination. It was discovered she had breast cancer. Surgery was performed.

"When she came home," he said, "I thought about quitting. She didn't want me to do that. She didn't want to change anything."

Bobbie was pregnant. The McMullens' third child, Jonathan, was born ten months ago. The other children are Ryan, 5, and Kenna, 3.

Bobbie McMullen died last April. She was 30. It was the opening day of the baseball season.

"I took off a few weeks to get the kids straightened away," he said. "Then I went back to work. I had to make a living. There was nothing else I could do."

For four months there were a series of baby sitters, friends, relatives, strangers, anybody who could take care of three small children.

"Then my sister, Andrea, and her husband, a student, decided they could live in my house and take care of the kids. They don't have any of their own. Maybe they won't want any after what they've been through."

McMullen's story was told early in the Los Angeles papers. There was much sympathetic mail from fans.

"Most people write and say they know how I feel," McMullen said. "Nobody knows how I feel."

The two other children were in school most of the season. McMullen would come home late from a night game, the sister would get the children off to school, he would sleep until noon and then he would play with them until 3 o'clock when he had to leave for the park.

"They'd rush through the door, say, 'Hi, Daddy,' and take off outside most of the time. You know how kids are. As long as their belly's full and they have a place to play, they're happy."

The season was long for McMullen, with Cey playing every day, and the adjustment of the children.

"It might have been easier if I were playing more. I would have been more occupied but I had to go on. I couldn't change things," he said.

In the days shortly after his wife's death, McMullen would journey with the children to the cemetery. He thought it was important.

"They would just run and play on the grass. It didn't mean anything to them. I stopped doing it. It didn't serve any purpose," he said.

McMullen found the road trips the most important part of the season for him.

"I had to get away," he said. "That was the only place I could really relax. For a while the guys wouldn't ask me to go out. They didn't want to do or say anything that would upset me. Then they realized things had to be as they were before. I've had a couple of dates now. I'm in no rush to remarry."

McMullen says the children sometimes mention their mother's name or ask about her or say they miss her.

"I try to explain to them about death," he said. "It's difficult. They are so small. I'm more concerned now with explaining to them about life."

McMullen says he is hopeful of getting a few more years of baseball in. A couple of years ago he would not have accepted his utility role so easily.

"I'm happy here," he said. "Cey is a hell of a young ballplayer. I know I'm not going to beat him out. I'll be happy to sit on the bench if they pay me what I'm worth."

Cey had gotten four hits, had hit a home run, had starred at third the other day in Pittsburgh, was surrounded by writers seeking out his thoughts.

McMullen's thoughts were easy to get, easy to understand.

"I guess I have a different outlook on baseball now," he said. "It's not that important. It used to be my life."

McMullen is looking forward to the end of this trying year.

"I'm going away someplace," he said, "just to rest and sleep and think. I have a lot of decisions to make."

33
MIKE JORGENSEN:
A DREAM FULFILLED

Before a player stays at first-class hotels and flies in huge jet planes, he usually spends some time in the minor leagues. This means bus trips over dusty roads, and hamburgers for lunch and supper.

Most players in the minors never get the thrill of playing on one of the major-league teams. Robert Lipsyte's story includes several of those who never made it to the bigs, but it includes Mike Jorgensen—who some say will develop into one of the game's superstars before he's finished. Jorgensen made it to the Mets and was traded to Montreal as part of the deal which brought Rusty Staub to New York.

By Robert Lipsyte

At twilight, when shadows flood the rolling Appalachian foothills, beyond center field, a chubby bank cashier mounts a knoll overlooking a splintery high-school ball park, turns on a crackling loudspeaker, and shouts:

"Welcome to Marion Stadium, home of the Mets, where the stars of tomorrow shine tonight."

A shirt-sleeved crowd of 965 stands and cheers as the Mets, there for a bluegrass summer, burst onto the field.

Dave Rose pounds his catcher's mitt just a little harder than usual—his parents are in the stands, down from Clarington, Ohio, to make sure their 17-year-old is getting his greens.

Phil Spyres, a 20-year-old from Tulsa, crouches at shortstop, a little tense. Even Mike Jorgensen, the $20,000 bonus first baseman from Bayside, Queens, feels it this night.

The man from the big club, Bob Scheffing, is watching, and they all remember what they were told a month ago, when they reported to the Rookie League.

"This is it, boys," the manager, Buddy Peterson, had said, "you're professionals now. And if you mess up here, there's no place to go."

They are professionals, on the lowest level of organized baseball, part of the burgeoning program to give high-school and college-age prospects a chance to polish fundamental skills before moving up into the more competitive environment of the minor leagues or out of baseball entirely.

The Marion club, in its second year of operation, is one of five community-owned, major-league-stocked-and-equipped teams in the Rookie League.

The starting pitcher, Don Linehan of Lorton, Virginia, gets into trouble right away, walking the first man in the Johnson City batting order. Johnson City is a New York Yankee club, scrambling to overtake the league-leading Mets. By the end of the first inning, the Yankees are leading 4-0, but Linehan is still pitching.

"In the minors," says Scheffing, a former big-league catcher and manager, now the New York Mets' director of player development, "the boy would have been relieved by now. We like to win games here, but we're more interested in finding out whether a boy can really play baseball, and whether he really wants to."

Scheffing makes a note to tell Linehan, at the next morning's instructional session, to spend more time warming up before a starting assignment, to throw as hard as he can the last five minutes before he takes the mound. Too many big-league games are lost in the early innings.

"We try to let a kid go as far as he can," says Scheffing, "whatever his position. That's for us, as well as them. Some of these boys from California and New York come here with a high gloss—a polish from good coaching and competition—while some small-town boys, who may have greater raw talent, don't look so good right away."

Scheffing and the manager, Peterson, are not the only ones watching the nine ball players with measuring eyes. In the dugout and bullpen, 30 other Marion Mets are comparing every on-field move with their own.

"There are two other shortstops here," says Barry Carter, a 19-year-old high-school senior from Chambersburg, Pennsylvania, "and we only get to play every third game. You sort of feel happy if another guy at your position makes an error or strikes out. I think it's natural, and it's nothing personal. And then you feel guilty for feeling happy, because he's trying to make it just as hard as you are."

The bank cashier, who is the club's president, Bob Garnett, announces the new Red Cross swimming program, then tells the crowd that one of last year's Marion Mets, now in the minor leagues, hit several home runs for Auburn the other night. The crowd cheers, because they knew him when he was hanging around Campbell's Restaurant and swimming at nearby Hungry Mother State Park.

"Next stop, Shea Stadium," someone yells.

Linehan has settled down now and the 17-year-old Jorgensen makes the score 4-2 with a 380-foot home run.

"Major-league homer," says Scheffing. "That boy is a prospect."

The Marion operation costs the Mets about $50,000

annually. Garnett's group, a nonprofit corporation, breaks even with its sale of tickets (50 cents each) and programs (10 cents and a pencil is included). The town—with 8,600 people dependent on a wooden plastics plant that gets defense contracts, a men's pajama factory and a state mental institution that employs 500—sees the team as added revenues for hotels, boarding houses, restaurants, clothing stores and car and bicycle dealers.

And, in an area that gets no regular baseball on television, the Marion Mets are entertainment and contact with glamor in the making.

For the boys, Marion is a low-pressure staging area, where concentrating on baseball is easy. There is no hard liquor, many of the teen-age girls leave town as soon as they can get bus fare, and the night life comprises two movie houses with early shows. But this is no summer camp. The boys are on their own.

"I was homesick at first," says the catcher from Clarington, Dave Rose. "Sundays were the worst. I really looked forward to Sunday at home, getting dressed, going to church, walking along the Ohio River with my girl. And, on Sunday, Mom always made chicken. She's a wonderful cook. And we had milk straight from the dairy; you should see the cream in that milk."

Now, Dave shares a house with three other players, washes his own clothes and dishes and makes himself chicken pot pies and beef stews out of cans.

Two 17-year-old catchers, Bob Yodice of Bensonhurst, Brooklyn, and Mike Minster of Los Angeles, share a trailer five miles from town. Yodice, who had observed how his mother did it at home, does the cleaning and cooking. Minster, who says he is "helpless around the house," seems very proud that he now picks up his own dirty underwear.

The boys agree that road trips (half of Marion's 60 games are played in other league towns) are the toughest part of the summer. The boys travel by bus, lodge in small-town hotels, and get $3 a day meal money on the road to supplement their average $400-a-month salary.

"If you're cheap," says Frank Lolich, a 20-year-old college senior from Portland, Oregon, "you can do one of two things. Eat only hamburgers for three meals, or sleep until it's time to go to the ball park. Mr. Peterson doesn't like us to stay in bed; he says it makes you lazy. And if you don't eat good food, you're only hurting yourself."

Only 21 players make each road trip, the others continuing the daily instructional sessions, where a catcher is taught never to make a target with his glove for the pitcher ("It's not the professional way"), and a baseman learns what to do when a runner, on a close play, tries to knock him down ("Tag him on the mouth").

It is at Marion, however, with the full squad watching and a crowd counting on them, that the Mets are tested. "Atta way to go," yells a kid in a Little League uniform as Carl Gentile, a little center fielder from St. Louis, makes a good catch.

"Small-town baseball, like it used to be," says Scheffing, "but not so good. That's part of it, too: getting along with folks, learning to act properly."

The Mets rally, and beat the Yankees, 7-6, and the crowd lingers in the dark stands as the boys make their way out of the park, up a flight of steps and over the knoll on the long climb to the crowded Marion Senior High School locker room.

For some of them, the season will end too soon, with a firm but gentle good-by from Buddy Peterson. Since most of them received bonuses or are assured college scholarships, the failure will dim quickly into a pocket of sweet nostalgia.

For others there will be other long steps, in Greenville, Auburn, Jacksonville, Williamsport, Buffalo—tougher towns than Marion, with better ball players closer to the top.

"Just before I left home, that last night," says Jorgensen, "I dreamed about having my own car, and living at home in Bayside, and commuting to work at Shea Stadium."

34
HANK AARON:
HE'S NUMBER ONE

This article by Al Silverman was written in 1958. Sixteen years later Hank Aaron moved past Babe Ruth and became the all-time home-run king of major-league baseball. At the start of the 1974 campaign it was expected that Aaron would retire when the season was over. However, he later announced that he wanted to play in 1975—as a member of the Milwaukee Brewers in the American League. The trade was arranged, and Aaron returned to the city where he began the career which placed him number one in nearly every offensive category. What better way to end this book than with a story about the greatest home-run king in history?

By Al Silverman

What do you want to know about Henry Aaron? Ask Don Newcombe, he'll tell you.

The bristling Dodger right-hander had kind of an off season last year but he's still one of the real good throwers in the game today. Ask Don Newcombe about Henry Aaron. He'll tell you.

This one happened in Milwaukee last summer. Don Newcombe was on the mound for the Dodgers and having a pretty fair time of it, except for Henry Aaron. In two previous times up, Aaron had doubled and been robbed of a hit. His third time up facing Newcombe, the count went to two strikes. Then Big Newk came in with a waste pitch, low and outside, which the book says is the way you should pitch to Aaron; let him fish for it. Henry fished all right, and connected, and the ball splattered into right center. Aaron landed on second base with his second double of the game.

Then the fun began.

With time called the burly Newcombe strode out to second base and aimed a few well-chosen words at Aaron. This extraordinary gesture on the part of an enemy ball-player was misinterpreted by the Milwaukee fans, who started booing Newcombe. But Hank just stood there at second base laughing and brushing off his uniform and laughing some more. Newcombe shuffled back to the mound talking to himself.

What had Newcombe said to Aaron out there? Henry was still laughing when he came back to the dressing room after the game. "He said to me, 'Next time I'm going to throw the blamed thing under the plate to you.'"

Ask Don Newcombe about Aaron. He'll tell you.

Ask those American League winners, the Yankees, about Aaron, too. They'll tell you—under their breath. In the seven-game World Series, Hank started off kind of slow, "fishing a little instead of waiting for my pitch," is how he put it. But he warmed up in time to finish with 11 hits, one less than the World Series record and high for both clubs; the most home runs (3); and the most runs batted in (7). While the Braves as a team were hitting a rather anemic .209, Hank's .393 was tops for both clubs. Ask the Yankees about Aaron. They'll tell you.

Ask the Braves themselves about Aaron; they'd be delighted to tell you. Manager Fred Haney: "The most relaxed hitter I've ever seen." Veteran Red Schoendienst: "The greatest right-handed hitter I've ever seen and he's got more power than the greatest left-hander, Musial."

The only one who won't talk about Henry Aaron (unless pressed) is Aaron himself. Ask Aaron about Aaron and you sometimes come away talking to yourself.

For instance, early this year Aaron was telling all who would listen that he was no home-run hitter, that if he hit in the low 30s, he'd be doing very well. Well, all the no-

home-run hitter did was lead both leagues in the number
of homers hit in 1957, 44; at the same time driving in the
most runs, 132. The batting title he had won a year earlier
was sacrificed to power—Hank was going after the long
ball for most of the season—and the sacrifice paid off in a
pennant, and then a world championship for the Milwaukee Braves.

His 43rd home run, incidentally, was the biggest hit of
his life. That was the one that gave the Braves the pennant. It came on September 23, against the challenging
second-place Cardinals, in the last of the 11th with the
score tied 2-2, two out and a runner on first. It earned outfielder Wes Covington the right to pour champagne over
Aaron's head in the dressing room after the game. It was,
said Aaron at the time, the biggest thrill of his life.

But he had others—four- and five-hit days, game-winning blows, etc.—and the slim, trim 24-year-old belter
who is regarded by most experts right now as the best hitter
in the league and likely to be the best hitter for years to
come, will enjoy many such days.

One nice trait of Aaron's is his impartiality as a bats-
man. In each of his four years in the majors Henry has hit
home runs in every National League ball park—and no
other major-leaguer, past or present, can make that state-
ment. Also in the last two years, he has hit home runs
against every club in the league, both at home and on the
road. As for his 132 RBIs, the significant thing about
that healthy total is that in 50 of the games he played in,
he batted in the unproductive second position. Hank had
another handicap, too, last year, in that he was forced to
play center field for half the season because of an injury to
the regular center fielder, Bill Bruton. Hank is a right
fielder by trade but he handled himself like a man in
center, although he is a long way from being a Willie
Mays as a fielder. "He doesn't look like he hustles out there
with that long loping gait of his," says Fred Haney, "but
you'll notice he always seems to get to a fly ball when
there's any chance of making it."

Because of his limitless potential, Aaron has been sub-
jected to as many words of advice and criticism as praise.

The experts see such a brilliant future in the young man that they almost automatically feel constrained to offer words of advice. It was the same with Ted Williams when he was a kid and batting over .400. The authorities still felt need to counsel him.

Rogers Hornsby, one of Aaron's milder critics, says that Aaron does have a weakness at bat—"a pitch with something on it right across the letters and in close." But Hornsby is quick to add that this is a batting weakness shared by every great hitter. Presumably, Hornsby was thinking about himself, too, because they don't come much greater.

Stan Musial, who staged a marvelous come-back last year to take away the hitting title from Aaron, once described the Braves greyhound-built outfielder as an "arrogant" hitter. "He thinks there's nothing he can't hit," says Musial, "but there's still some pitches no hitter can afford to go for."

Aaron is generally considered to be a bad-ball hitter—the saying goes that he's the best bad-ball hitter to come along in the National League since Joe Medwick. "Sure he's a bad-ball hitter," says Bobby Bragan, who had ample opportunity to observe Aaron when Bragan was managing the Pirates. "It would be a bad mistake to change him, though," Bragan thinks.

When Aaron first came up to the majors his philosophy of batting was stated this way: "I just go up swinging. I like to swing at everything that looks good to me." Now it's different. Today he says, "I wait for my pitch," and that is, after all, the measure of a new maturity in the man.

Even though Aaron was swinging for the long ball last year, he might still have won the batting title (he finally finished fourth in the league with a .322 average) if it weren't for the isolated times when he began to press and lash out at everything instead of waiting for his pitch. The circumstance that perhaps hurt him the most came late in the season when he made some unfortunate public remarks to the effect that a certain St. Louis pitcher, among others, was throwing in the general direction of his noggin. To be perfectly fair to Hank, the accusation was made when the Braves were laboring hard and faltering a bit in their pennant efforts. And much of the hitting burden at the time was on Aaron. For quite a few games after that, Hank had trouble regaining his stride, as if the weight of his remarks had laid a heavy hand on his bat.

At any rate, if there is one thing that Aaron is not, it is a pop-off artist. In fact since coming to the majors, he's earned a reputation for his reticence and for his sparseness of conversation, which is not altogether justified, either. While Aaron is no pop-off, neither is he a primitive.

Mr. Aaron of Mobile, Alabama (the town gave him a whopping welcome-home reception after the World Series, choosing to ignore the fact that he now makes his home in Milwaukee), is an undistinguished figure in a baseball uniform. He stand 5-11½, weighs 175 and everybody wonders how he gets the power to hit to all fields the way he does. When he moves from the ondeck circle to the batter's box, he does so in indolent fashion, loping along slowly on bouncy heels. Once he is set in the box, he gives the impression of being rather bored with life. But when the pitcher gets set to fire the ball, Aaron is ready. "He may not look it," says Fred Haney, "but he's always ready to hit. Ever notice how he holds that bat away from him? You have to be a great wrist hitter to do that in the big leagues."

Most baseball experts agree that Aaron has the best wrists in the game today. It is the wrist action, along with the power in his forearms, plus perfect eyesight and an uncanny sense of timing that makes Aaron the best hitter in baseball. Teammate Warren Spahn once remarked how amazing it was to see Aaron stand there and wait for a pitch before making up his mind about swinging. "It's like giving him an extra strike," Spahn says in awe.

Since jumping from Class A baseball to the majors in 1954 (a feat of considerable dimensions in this day and age) all Aaron has done is take his place directly behind Stan Musial in the matter of active National League players with the best lifetime hitting percentage. His first year up with the Braves Henry hit a respectable .280. In 1955 he jumped to .314, including 27 home runs and 106 runs batted in. And in 1956 his league-leading average was .328, with 26 homers and 92 RBIs. He was the only major-leaguer to get 200 hits that year. Last year his 198 hits were two behind the major-league pace-setter, teammate Red Schoendienst.

Ever since he was a kid watching the big-league ballclubs sneak into Mobile for a day on their way north from Florida, Henry hungered for the time he would be traveling with them, as a major-leaguer. Later when he became a member of the Braves, and presumably more sophisticated, he set three other goals for himself—to win the most-valuable-player award (which he did in 1957), to lead his league in hitting, to play in a World Series. Today only 24 years old, Henry Aaron has come just about as close as any man in attaining his aims in life.

Henry is the third oldest boy in a family of eight that includes four older brothers and three sisters. His father, who was a shipbuilder worker in Mobile, also did some ballplaying on the side, but he wasn't playing much ball when Henry was born, February 5, 1934, in the shank of the depression.

In his sandlot days in Mobile, Aaron started out as a catcher, then switched to shortstop—he was always a hitter. He played shortstop for his Central High softball team (the school couldn't afford the equipment for baseball) and also starred in football. When he graduated from Central High at age 17 he played semipro ball with the local Negro baseball team. One day the big-city Indianapolis Clowns came in for an exhibition and the 150-pound Aaron rapped three hits. The Clowns, being a practical aggregation, took the local youngster with them.

But they didn't hold onto their prodigy long. Henry was batting about .450 that early summer of 1952 and the scouts began converging on Sid Pollet, the Clowns owner. Pollet had all but completed a deal for Aaron to play for the Giants' farm at Sioux City, Iowa, when Dewey Griggs, the Braves scout, happened along. He won Aaron's hand. "The Giants wanted to give me an A contract and a C salary," is how Hank explains his signing with the Braves. He reported directly to Eau Claire in the Northern League and in 87 games established himself as a comer. He hit

.336, was named league all-star shortstop and was voted rookie of the year.

The next year with Jacksonville in the Class A Sally League, Aaron completed his lower education. This is what he did for Ben Geraghty's pennant-winning team: Lead the league in hits (208); runs (115); runs batted in (125); average (.362); putouts and assists. He also hit 22 home runs and was second in the league in triples. Naturally, he won the league's most-valuable-player award hands down. "It was," said Ben Geraghty, "one of the greatest one-man performances I ever saw. Henry just stood up there flicking those great wrists of his and simply overpowered the pitching."

The next year the Braves figured that if Aaron made it to Triple A he would be accomplishing something. After all, he was just 20 years old, with but two years of minor-league seasoning behind him. The front office ticketed him for their Toledo American Association club, but in the spring he went to Bradenton, Florida, to work out with the old pros. There he proved among other things he was also an opportunist.

Henry had played winter ball in Puerto Rico and had his eye when he reported to the Braves in the spring of '54. The Braves put Aaron in the outfield. They figured he would never make it as a shortstop in the majors. Aaron said at the time that it was all right with him because it meant he wouldn't have to do as much thinking (he likes to give people the impression, slightly erroneous, that he isn't a thinking man). Henry hit well all spring and then when the newly acquired Bobby Thomson broke his ankle, the way was clear for Aaron to stay up with the Braves. He had a fine season, finishing second to Wally Moon in the voting for Rookie of the Year. He might have caught Moon in the stretch because he was coming on as a hitter when he got into an accident. Playing a double-header late in the season he collected five straight hits. On the fifth hit he slid into third base and broke his ankle. But the fracture did nothing more than postpone the inevitable, which came in 1955—the establishment of Henry Aaron as an uncommonly gifted ballplayer.

Hank is married to the former Barbara Lucas and the Aarons have two children, Gail Elaine, who is five, and Hank, Jr., ten months. Henry moved to Milwaukee over the winter to accept a public-relations job with a local brewery, along with some of his Braves teammates.

He should do all right in the public-relations line. Off the field, Henry is a very friendly young man who likes to swim and play pool and eat seafood, especially shrimp. He has a good sense of humor, although it ordinarily has to be drawn out of him because he doesn't care to talk unless spoken to. Teammate Del Crandall describes Aaron as being "dumb as a fox." Once in his rookie year Aaron hit a home run against Robin Roberts and when he returned to the bench he exclaimed in wonder, "Is that really Roberts out there?"

Another time in the off season he was attending a banquet when the Braves' boss Lou Perini got up and in the course of things began extolling the virtues of Henry Aaron. Henry, who looked as if he was dozing through the speech, nudged teammate Bill Bruton and whispered, "Does he mean that before or after I sign?"

One of Hank's lengthiest declamations came when he hit that pennant-winning home run against the Cardinals. Sitting in the dressing room after the game, Milwaukee's good beer sopping through his uniform, he said, "My first thought was Bobby Thomson's homer. That's always been my idea of the most important homer. Now I got one myself. For me to get the hit myself—am I excited! I'm excited for the first time in my life!"